HAT TRICK

KELLY JAMIESON

PRAISE FOR THE NOVELS OF KELLY JAMIESON

"Jamieson creates an emotionally complex, well-written story about relationships."

—RT Book Reviews

"Ms. Jamieson is rapidly becoming one of my favorite authors."

—Just Erotic Romance Reviews

"Her characters are intelligent, believable and heartwarming."

—Night Owl Reviews

"Ms. Jamieson once again gives the reader a richly detailed story that is brimming over with sexual tension, intoxicating desires and intriguing carnal needs that is edgy and psychologically intense..."

—The Romance Studio

"...I love Kelly Jamieson's books and the way that she depicts her characters..."

—*Sizzling Hot Book Reviews*

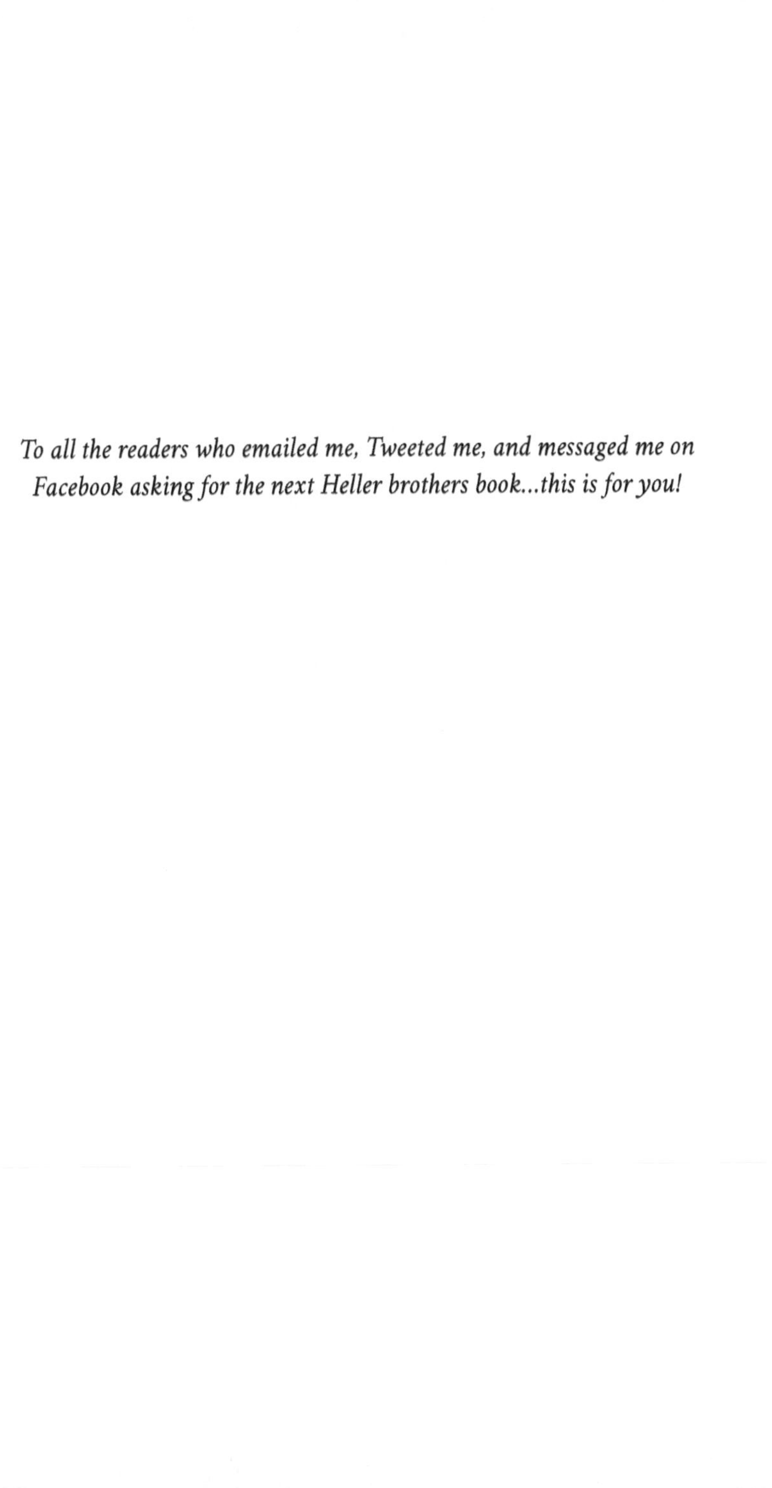

To all the readers who emailed me, Tweeted me, and messaged me on Facebook asking for the next Heller brothers book...this is for you!

CHAPTER ONE

"I told the designer I wanted counters that were the right height for fucking."

Remi choked on a laugh, sitting on the granite countertop of the big kitchen island where Jase had picked her up and set her. She followed his gaze down to where their bodies met, her thighs spread and him standing between them, her pussy against his bulging crotch. Arousal tightened inside her. "Did you seriously plan that?"

He grinned and nipped at her chin. "Maybe."

"Well, the new kitchen looks great."

"I think so too."

This was the house Remi had grown up in, the house she and her siblings had inherited when their parents died. Jase had bought it when she'd been forced to put it on the market so she could pay her brother and sister their share of its value, a gesture so sweet and generous it had made her cry. He'd intended for her to continue living there, but when she'd decided she wanted to move into her own apartment, he'd moved into the house himself.

"You've put so much work into this house."

"I like this house. I told you, it reminds me of my parents' house in Winnipeg."

Arms draped over his shoulders, she smiled and combed her fingers through his hair. He'd taken her to visit his parents this past summer. They'd spent time in his home city and at the lake, and she'd gotten to know his family better. His parents and all three of his brothers had been home for various parts of the summer. She'd loved spending time with them and seeing where Jase had grown up.

"And it's a good family home," he said. "But what I really want is you here living with me."

Her mouth softened. "I want that too."

"Then move back. Move in with me. We can spend our first Christmas together here."

"We're going to Winnipeg for Christmas."

"Well, yeah. But just for a couple of days. There's only a four-day break in the schedule for me." Jase played in the National Hockey League. "We can get a tree, and have Christmas here too. Come on, Remi."

She bit her lip.

"I know you feel bad about leaving your brother and sister alone at Christmas. We could do something here with them to celebrate."

"We can do that anyway," she pointed out. "I don't have to be living here for that."

"Ah, Remi. I know you're trying to prove you can do this—cut your brother and sister loose and just live for yourself. But you don't need to live alone in that little apartment to do it. You can do it here with me. And it's crazy for you to pay rent when you don't have to."

"It's my money," she muttered, giving his shoulder a little shove. He had more money than he knew what to do with, and her insistence on supporting herself frustrated him.

"I know, baby."

"My little apartment just isn't up to your standards."

"Hey, I'm not that spoiled." He grinned.

"You totally are. Look at this kitchen." She swept one arm out. "Custom-made maple cabinets. Granite counters. Sub-Zero built-in refrigerator to match the cupboards. *Two* ovens *and* a microwave. Even the knobs on the drawers are high-end. You didn't care how much this cost. Same with the bathroom renos and the new roof and the new patio and sidewalk and…"

"It's what I wanted."

The renos hadn't even put a dent in his bank account. The house she'd grown up in had been overtaken by teams of designers, contractors and tradespeople, Jase sparing no expense in making the old house like new again, while carefully preserving the character and charm of the original structure.

She smiled, shaking her head. "Admit it. You had fun working with the designer."

He sifted his fingers through her hair and sensation shimmered over her. She loved it when he touched her hair, which he did a lot. She loved it when he touched her, period. "Fine. I admit it. It's been fun." He met her eyes. "But the point isn't whether your apartment is good enough. The point is, I want you here with me."

Aw. It was so hard to refuse when she loved him so much.

Her purse sitting on the counter began to chime, and they both turned to look at it.

She smiled and Jase stretched an arm out to grab it and bring it closer. She pulled her cell phone out and looked at the screen. Speaking of her younger sister… "It's Jasmine." She clicked the talk button. "Hey, Jas."

"Remi." Jasmine's tear-thickened voice made Remi's heart plunge. "Where are you?"

"I'm at the house. Jase's house," she clarified. Although Jasmine would know which house she meant. "Helping him put things away in the new kitchen."

"Can I come over?" Jasmine sniffed. "I need to talk to you."

Remi sighed. "What's wrong, Jas? Did you and Ethan have another fight?"

"Sort of."

Remi met Jase's eyes which were watching her steadily. "Come on over," she said.

"Okay. Thanks."

Remi ended the call and set the phone down. "Sorry. Sounds like more trouble in paradise."

Jase snorted. "I'd hardly call it paradise. More like hell."

"I know." She shook her head. "I wasn't happy when they moved in together, and things don't seem to be any better. But she was determined they were going to live together."

"She's twenty-one. An adult."

"But a young adult."

"True." Jase held up a hand. "And don't start with the self-blame. You're not responsible for her immaturity."

She gave him a glum smile. "Thank you, but you know I feel like I am."

He set his hands on her waist. "You may have been a little too easy on her sometimes, but it's because you love her."

Remi laughed. "There are times I wonder why. But yeah, you're right." She'd been responsible for her younger siblings after their parents' death, and she loved them and wanted to do everything she could for them, but she knew now that she might have had a tendency to make things a little too easy for them. She was trying hard to let them make their own mistakes without stepping in to bail them out.

He leaned in and gave her a soft smooch on the lips. "Whatever's going on with her now, I'm here for you."

"Thank you." Her heart squeezed with love for him. She slid a hand around the back of his neck, into his short hair, and kissed him back. "Now help me down from here so I can get back to work."

He held her by the waist and lifted her down as if she weighed as much as a bag of flour. She was on vacation from her teaching job for the next two weeks, until after New Years. The kitchen reno complete, they now had boxes of dishes and glasses and cutlery and food to unpack and put away, although Jase didn't have a lot of kitchen stuff. She spent the next half hour unpacking boxes, until the doorbell rang. With some amusement, Remi went to answer the door. Jase had changed the locks and Jasmine's key no longer worked. Hey, it was his house now.

Jasmine had definitely been crying, judging from the puffy eyes and pink nose.

"Aw, honey, are you okay?" Remi asked, taking her younger sister's jacket and scarf. Jasmine toed off her Ugg boots and then padded behind Remi into the kitchen again.

"Not really." Jasmine gave a little sniffle. "Oh wow. Look at the kitchen." She stood in the door and surveyed the room. The she burst into tears.

Remi's eyes met Jase's. She sighed and moved over to her sister to hug her. "C'mere and have a seat," Remi invited, indicating one of the stools at the new granite-topped island. "Do you want some coffee? Tea? Hot chocolate?"

Jasmine gave another huge sniffle. "Tea would be good."

"Hmm. I don't know where the kettle is, but I can put a mug in the microwave. Jase, you want any?"

He lifted an eyebrow. "Tea? Uh. No thanks, babe."

She hid her smile. "Just asking."

"Hi, Jasmine," Jase said, standing there collapsing a cardboard box.

"Hi, Jase."

Remi busied herself making a couple of mugs of tea. "So what's going on?" she asked Jasmine gently.

Jasmine gave a gusty sigh. "I'm so pissed off at Ethan!"

Remi nodded and resisted the urge to roll her eyes. She leaned against the counter as the mugs of water heated in the microwave. "Why?"

"I want to redo our kitchen and he says we can't." She threw out a hand. "Look at this! Our kitchen is so dumpy compared to this!"

"You just moved in," Remi reminded her. "And your kitchen is not a dump."

The reason Jasmine had wanted Remi to sell the house was so she could have her share of the money and use it to buy a house for her and Ethan. Remi'd been concerned about that, but Jase was right, Jasmine was an adult, and she'd resented Remi's hesitations and dismissed her worries about her relationship with Ethan. Together she and her boyfriend had purchased a small house not too far away, a house that definitely needed some updating, but even so it had cost more than Remi'd thought they should spend. Remi wasn't sure how handy Ethan was and hoped they weren't going to have to spend a lot of money to hire people to do the updates they needed done.

"It is a dump. It's embarrassing to have people over." She gazed around at the expensive appliances, new cupboards and shiny counters. She looked at Remi. "There are so many things that need to be done in the house and Ethan says we can't afford them."

Remi wasn't sure what to say to that. "Well. Home renovations are expensive, unless you can do them yourselves."

"Even then, they're expensive," Jase said, moving to sit on another stool at the island. "You still have to pay for materials."

Jasmine gave him a look. "I'm sure you didn't do any of this yourself."

Jase returned her look steadily. "No. I didn't. But I can afford to pay people to do it."

"You don't have to brag," she muttered. "I know how rich you are."

"Jasmine!" Remi stared at her sister.

"Sorry. I didn't mean that the way it sounded. I'm just frustrated. I don't like living in that shabby little house and Ethan apparently can't even hammer a nail."

The microwave beeped and Remi pulled the two mugs out and dropped tea bags into them. She nibbled her bottom lip. "He could probably learn. Some of the big home stores put on do-it-yourself classes. I went to a few when I needed to know how to fix a leaky tap or how to paint a room."

"Huh. Maybe." Jasmine's eyebrows joined above her nose. "But what are we supposed to do in the meantime? He can't do it himself and we can't afford to pay someone to do it."

"Maybe that means living there for a while the way it is," Jase offered.

Jasmine looked down at the counter glumly. "I don't want to."

"Then why did you buy the house?" he asked in a neutral voice.

Jasmine huffed. "It was all we could afford."

"Maybe you need to adjust your expectations."

"Easy for you to say." Jasmine pouted.

Remi wasn't sure where this was going. Did Jasmine actually think Jase was going to give them money? Because, holy crap, she had another think coming if that was the case.

"Jasmine," she said carefully. "Did you just want to vent about things? Or do you want us to do something to help? Because I'm not sure there's anything we can do."

Jasmine blinked wetly. "I-I want sell the house. Our mortgage payment is so big, we can't afford to do anything else, and we can't afford to renovate it. All our friends are going to Puerto Vallarta in January and we can't go with them."

"Ah." Remi again met Jase's eyes. His lips quirked but the warmth in his eyes steadied her. "What friends are those?"

"Leah and Brent, and Jen and Paul."

"They all still live at home with their parents."

"Yeah."

"But you were pretty determined you and Ethan wanted to buy a house."

"I was, but...I know what you're going to say! You're totally going to say I told you so. But it's not like that."

"You made a big commitment, Jasmine. You wanted me to sell the house so you'd have enough to buy one of your own, but you only owned a third of this house. Did you really think you'd be able to move into something the same? And not have a mortgage?"

"No! I knew what I was doing. It's just not working out. And Ethan's not helping. I want to move back with you, Remi."

That gave Remi a jolt. "I don't have room in my apartment," she said slowly. "There's barely room for me, never mind someone else."

Jasmine sighed. "Shit." Then she looked around. "But there's lots of room here." She looked at Jase expectantly. "I could stay here."

Remi looked at Jase. He gave her a crooked smile. "There's room here," he agreed pleasantly. Remi blinked. "But you'd have to pay rent."

Jasmine frowned. "Get out of here. Seriously?"

"Seriously."

"But I'm practically your family," Jasmine said. "Practically your sister-in-law."

"True," Jase agreed. "But your sister sacrificed a lot for you, because you wanted to buy a house and move in with your boyfriend, and you need to deal with the consequences of that."

Remi breathed in through her nose to stop the tears that stung her eyes. Her heart swelled with love for Jase. She bent her head to remove the tea bags from the cups, blinking hard.

"He's right, Jasmine." She set a mug on the island in front of her sister. "Sorry."

If it was really, really urgent, like if it was a matter of Jasmine being homeless and sleeping on the streets, she could make room for her and let her sleep on her couch. Long term, maybe not, but short term, sure. But this wasn't a matter of Jasmine being homeless, this was a matter of Jasmine being spoiled and immature. And once again, Remi experienced a pang of guilt at her role in making Jasmine this way.

"You need to talk to Ethan," she said gently, picking up her own mug of steaming tea. "If you really want out, you have to discuss it with him. You both own that house." She swallowed another sigh, painfully aware that Jasmine had contributed much more toward the purchase of the house than Ethan had. "I sold this house so you could do that. I moved into a little apartment —"

"You didn't have to!" Jasmine burst out. "Jason bought this house! You could be living here right now."

Once again, Remi and Jase exchanged a look of understanding. Yes, she could be. Jase understood why she wasn't, even though he wanted her there. Clearly, Jasmine didn't get it, and Remi wasn't going to try to explain it.

She *wanted* to live with Jase. They practically did anyway, and it was getting to be a pain going back and forth between this place and her apartment. With his six foot three inches and two hundred ten pounds, he seemed to fill up her little one-bedroom apartment.

But she'd actually enjoyed having her very own place for the first time in her life, enjoying the freedom and lack of responsibility she'd never before experienced. Even before her parents had died, she'd been the one who'd looked after Jasmine and Kyle when their parents were away on their frequent trips. And now dating a rich and famous hockey player, it would be easy to become "Jase Heller's girlfriend", easy to let him take care of her and do everything for her, but she wanted to be her own person.

"The fact remains," she continued. "You made decisions and you need to deal with them. Like an adult. If you don't want to live with Ethan anymore, then you're going to have find somewhere else to live, somewhere that you can afford."

Jasmine turned pleading eyes on Jase. "Jason, you don't need the rent money."

He lifted an eyebrow. "Nope."

"So let me move back here."

Remi almost held her breath, waiting for his answer. It was hard for her to say no. Thinking of her little sister unhappy was difficult. But she was seeing Jasmine more clearly now than she ever had and it was getting easier to say no to her. Because it really was for her own good. But Jason...? She glanced at him.

"Nope," he said again, easily. "Sorry, kiddo. Remi's right. You have to talk to Ethan and figure this out on your own."

It'd be a whole different hockey game if there'd been something seriously wrong, such as if Jasmine had even hinted that maybe Ethan was abusive in any way. But apparently this was just Jasmine being her flighty self. And that had to change.

She met Jase's eyes and they smiled at each other, slow and sweet and steady. She didn't try to hide the love she felt for him, and she could tell he got it. If it wasn't for him, she might never have gotten to this point. Which was kind of funny, because when they'd met, they'd both just been looking for fun. She was the one who'd always been the responsible adult, whereas he played a game for a living, but he was the one who'd helped her grow up just a little more. Her heart expanded hard against her breastbone, taking her breath away.

"Fine," Jasmine muttered, sliding off the stool. "I'll go talk to Ethan."

Remi dragged her gaze away from Jase's warm one with difficulty. God, she loved him. She shot him a what-can-you-do smile as she followed Jasmine to the door.

As Jasmine donned her jacket and boots, Remi said in a low voice, "I don't ever want to hear you talk to Jase like that again.

And I definitely never, *ever* want to even hear *hints* that you want him to pay for something for you."

Jasmine almost looked like she wanted to roll her eyes, but luckily she appeared to think better of that, and instead Remi thought she almost looked ashamed. "Yeah, I get it," she said. "Sorry."

Maybe there was hope for her.

CHAPTER TWO

"I think she's afraid of me," Jase said when Remi returned moments later, Jasmine gone.

Remi laughed as he pulled her into his arms. She was so little and soft, but he loved how she felt next to him.

"What? I can be a scary dude."

"Well." She smoothed a hand over his shoulder. "You are pretty big." She looked up at him through her eyelashes, her pretty turquoise eyes all shiny and sexy. "But *I'm* not afraid of you."

"No." He pulled her a little closer. "You never have been, have you?" The first few times they'd had sex, he'd been the one who was afraid—afraid of hurting her because she was small and he was big and he liked sex the way he played hockey—hard, fast and physical. But they'd discovered she liked sex that way too.

"And Kyle is coming around too," Jason added, bending to kiss her cheek and nuzzle her ear. She shivered.

"I can't believe she did that," she said. "I'm so sorry, Jase. I can't believe she thought she could take advantage of your money. God!" She closed her eyes. "She's so spoiled! And I'm the one who did that to her."

"There you go blaming yourself again. Seriously, Rem. It's not all your fault. She's young and yeah, maybe she had life a little too easy sometimes, but not everyone ends up ungrateful like that. Kyle's not like that. I've seen how he appreciates what you've done. I think it's just part of her personality."

She nodded, eyes still closed, mouth clamped shut.

"You know I'd do anything for your family," he continued in a low voice. "If they really needed something. Anything. I don't want you to think I'm being a cheap prick." For a moment, the idea of paying for a trip to Puerto Vallarta for Jasmine and Ethan as their Christmas present had entered his head, but he knew that wasn't the right thing to do.

She choked on a laugh. "God, no. I know you would, Jase. Thank you for backing me up with her. That's worth more than anything. I love you so much."

"Love you too, baby." His hands slid around her ass and pulled her closer to kiss her again. Her fingers played in his short hair. He made a rough sound as pleasure trickled down his spine. "Wanna go out for dinner?" he asked.

"I'd like to cook something here in this beautiful new kitchen. Let's just stay in. But we need to put the rest of this stuff away."

He gave her a lingering kiss then released her. They each went to work on a box.

"We need to make a trip to IKEA for you," she said.

"Or you could move in and bring all your stuff back here."

She smiled and shook her head at his persistent efforts to get her to move in with him. He grinned. He knew it would happen someday.

"Think how much harder it would have been for me to say no to her moving in with me if I was living here," she said. "I couldn't use the 'not enough room' excuse."

"True."

Remi lifted a set of four wineglasses out of a box and set them on the counter. "Oh. I bought some wine. It's in the fridge. Could you open it? I'll start dinner. We have some chicken breasts, and I'll see what else." She moved to the refrigerator.

As he helped Remi make dinner, they talked about their upcoming trip to Winnipeg, the big family Christmas his mom had planned since all four sons were living so close to home now. Three of them played in the NHL—Tag right there in Winnipeg, Logan in Minneapolis, a short one-hour flight away, and Jase here in Chicago, not that much farther. His youngest brother Matt was a student on a hockey scholarship at the University of North Dakota, only a two-hour drive away from Winnipeg in Grand Forks. Their schedules had all worked out that they could get together for a few days, so it would be a short trip, but it had been quite a few Christmases since the whole Heller family had all been together.

After dinner, they watched a movie, Remi snuggled in against him on the couch in front of the big television he'd moved in. As often happened, she started dozing off on his chest while they watched the movie, and when it ended, Jase gave her a gentle nudge. "Bed, hon."

She made the soft little sleep noises he found so cute, and sat up blinking and pushing her silky blonde hair off her face. "Sorry," she mumbled.

"Come on. You're staying here tonight." He clicked off the TV and the lamp, then picked her up and carried her up the stairs. She was such a little thing, it wasn't hard. It was still funny to him that he'd fallen so hard for a girl who wasn't even close to his type, which used to be tall girls with bigger chests, but fallen he had. Hard.

His bedroom had been Remi's parents' room at one time, which had freaked him out a little, but it was the only room in the house big enough for his king-size bed. He'd had the room completely redone and it looked nothing like it had before.

"There you go, babe," he said, setting her on her feet on the rug beside the bed. He flicked on the lamp, then reached for her.

His fingers went to the button of her jeans. Biting her lip, she lifted the hem of the turtleneck sweater she wore and pulled it up and over her head. His gaze lowered to her breasts. "Nice. My favorite bra."

He loved black lace and so now Remi had an extensive wardrobe of black lace lingerie. Only whereas she used to buy things from Victoria's Secret, Jase like to shop at Agent Provocateur and other expensive Chicago boutiques. This one was sheer black lace with a tiny scalloped-edge trim, cut scandalously low so it almost showed her nipples. She used to wear maximum push-up styles, but he liked things sheer. When she'd complained about her less-than-generous cleavage, he'd told her he loved her cleavage, and he didn't want to feel padding, he wanted to feel *her*.

He picked her up and sat her on the side of the big bed, kneeling before her to work the skinny jeans off her legs. Then he smiled as she sat there in sheer bra and thong panties—and thick black socks. He gently lifted each foot and tugged the socks off too. She leaned back on her elbows on the bed, pushing out her sweet little tits in the sheer bra.

"Fuck, that's hot."

Her tongue swept over her bottom lip and he let out a groan. He rose up over her and bent forward to press kisses between her breasts. Her eyes closed and her head fell back as his tongue traced the scalloped edge of the lace bra. Then he licked her nipple through the sheer fabric. Her body twitched.

He kissed his way down her body, over her belly, to the sheer black triangle at the apex of her thighs. He pressed a kiss there too, then set his big hands on her thighs and pushed them gently apart. He stroked his hands up and down her thighs, and she quivered as he nuzzled her pussy through filmy fabric. He breathed in her scent, delicate and feminine and aroused. Christ, it almost made him feel drunk, filling his head.

"Mmm. So sweet," he murmured. "Just wanna feast on you, baby."

"Jase."

He kissed her thighs, his eyes drifting closed, rubbed his cheek against her leg, kissed all the way down to her knee. Lifting her leg, he licked behind her knee where he knew she was so sensitive. Her sharply indrawn breath was his reward and he smiled against her soft skin.

She gave up trying to watch and collapsed flat on the bed. He kissed the inside of one knee, then the other, taking his time licking and kissing his way back to the center of her.

"You smell so good," he murmured, again nuzzling her panties. "You must be wet."

She moaned.

He tugged the panties off and she pushed her feet into the edge of the mattress to lift her hips. She dragged her eyes open and lifted her chin to look at him. "Take your clothes off too."

He smiled. "Not yet."

Bending again, he set his hands on her thighs and held her legs as his mouth descended to her core. He pressed soft kisses to her folds, gentle suckling kisses, up and down, moving to her inner thighs and then even lower as he pushed her legs higher and nipped at her butt cheeks. She lifted her hips against his mouth. "Jase, oh god."

His tongue came out and licked then, teasing over her skin, then dipping deeper, parting her folds, seeking out the center where she was hot and liquid. The delicate spice taste of her arousal slid over his tongue. "Mmm. Taste so good, Remi. Wanna lick you all over."

"God, you're good at this," she moaned. Warmth expanded inside him, knowing he was giving her pleasure.

He licked all over her pussy, his face pressed there between her legs, and then his tongue circled her clit. She made a soft sound of need, her hands fisted in the bedspread. Pressure and need built inside him, but he kept teasing her. When he finally licked over her clit, her whole body jolted.

"There," he murmured. "Like that?"

"You know I do," she panted, pulsing against his mouth, her hips lifting involuntarily.

"I like it too." And then he drew back and touched her, his big fingertips sliding over her. "Wanna play with this pretty pussy all night." Once more she tried to lift her head to look. He met her eyes then dropped his gaze to focus on her sex, and slid a finger inside her. Her pussy flexed and clenched around it. "Touching you like this. Tasting you like this." And he swept his tongue over her swollen clit, making her entire body tremble again.

He made another sound of appreciation low in his throat and again closed his eyes.

"Jase," she gasped."I'm going to come."

"Good."

"Want you inside me. Stop. Stop." She reached for his head.

He lifted his head and smiled at her, then wiped a hand across his wet mouth. "Okay, babe." In seconds, he had his fly undone, his jeans shoved down and his cock out, and she stared in fascination. Her lips parted hungrily.

"Oh babe, when you look at me like that I want your lips around my cock." His cock was on fire, heat rushing through his body.

She dragged her tongue over bottom lip and Jase groaned. He stripped his long-sleeved tee over his head and tossed it to the floor.

"Now," he growled. He picked her up and hauled her farther onto the bed, still sideways, then came down over her. He spread his knees wider, nudging her thighs apart, fisted his cock and slid the head up and down her pussy. "Oh yeah. So wet, Rem." He pushed into her, stretching her, and her body arched to take him deep. When he was in, all the way in, their bodies joined so intimately, he paused. He held himself there, deep inside her, pulsing. He looked down at her and their eyes met.

A moment passed, a long, lovely moment of sweetness and love. Hot sensation swelled in his chest. She stretched out her arms and reached for him, and he bent over her to claim her mouth with his. He released his hold on her legs and she wrapped them around him as they kissed, and held onto his shoulders.

Her body tightened, pulsating around him. "Jase. Please. So close…" Her body strained against his, and still he didn't move, so close himself. His balls grew tight at the base of his cock, pressed against her softness, pressure building inside him, his blood pumping through his veins. The muscles of his shoulders and arms bunched.

He touched her face, kissed her mouth, her cheek, her ear. And then he pulled out slowly, in an exquisite and excruciating drag of wet flesh, and pushed back in just as slowly. She gave a soft wail and he captured her mouth again, and this time when he slid out and pushed back in, it was harder, then harder still, faster. He felt her orgasm, her pussy rippling around him and she clung to him as he drove into her, finding his own release. A bolt of electricity seared up his spine, making his head buzz, then sizzled back down to his balls and out of his dick in hard spasms. He gave a long, low growl and went still, his body taut.

"Fuck," he muttered against her ear. "Fuck, that's good."

"Mmm."

They didn't move for long moments, both of them panting, hearts thudding against each other. "God I love you, Remi. Love you so much."

In the morning, Jase got up and left for practice early and Remi slept in. She finally climbed out of bed feeling deliciously well-rested and went down to the kitchen. Wintry sunshine filled the room and she again smiled and sighed over how beautiful it was.

Which reminded her of the scene with Jasmine yesterday. Her smile disappeared as she made herself coffee. Hopefully Jasmine had gone home and had an adult conversation with Ethan. Remi'd never been fond of Ethan, always feeling like he'd used Jasmine's immaturity and insecurities as a way to control her, which had often hurt her, but attempts to talk to Jasmine about that had not gone over well.

The back door opened and Jase stepped into the kitchen from the mud room, his hair still damp, his face still flushed with the workout he'd just had. His smile beamed at her when he saw her. "Hey, baby."

"Hi."

She moved across the kitchen to hug him. His cheeks were cold and so were his hands when he deliberately slipped them under her sweater, making her squeal. He laughed and kissed her mouth.

"How was practice?"

"Good. Mmm. Coffee." He moved toward the coffeemaker on the counter.

He'd been awesome yesterday with Jasmine. He was always awesome.

He'd make a good dad.

Oh yeah—he *was* a dad. Of a baby with another woman. A heavy sigh escaped her.

"What's wrong?" he asked, looking up from the mug he'd just filled with coffee.

Sometimes she managed to forget about that, but when memory returned it was always accompanied by a sick feeling and a dip in her mood. She hated to bring it up.

"You should get the DNA test results soon. Maybe even today."

His eyes shadowed and his lips tightened. "Yeah."

He hadn't even wanted to do the paternity test. Thank god his family had pressured him into it. She'd so wanted him to get the test done, but hadn't wanted to push. It would be easy to come across as jealous and insecure. Oh wait...she *was* jealous and insecure. But she was working really hard at not being that girl.

She and Jase had started seeing each other soon after his breakup with Brianne, his ex-girlfriend, fallen in love, and their world had seemed pretty perfect until Brianne dropped the bomb about the pregnancy a couple of months later. She'd insisted he was the father, and it was possible, given the timing.

But it had almost ended things between them. It hurt like hell to think of him having a baby with another woman, and especially when all her life she'd wanted to be a mother. She loved kids, hence the teaching career. And Jase had struggled too with the idea of burdening her with another woman's child in their lives. But they were getting through it, knowing things wouldn't be easy.

There'd always been that doubt in Remi's mind, though—the possibility that Jase wasn't the father. At first, he hadn't even believed Brianne was pregnant. He'd thought she was just trying to get back together. But now there was a little baby girl named Emily, who Brianne was being pretty protective of, despite Jase's determination to do the right thing and be a good father to his child. He was so determined to do the right thing he hadn't even wanted to have the paternity test done.

"It'll be okay," she said to him with a determinedly reassuring smile. "Whatever happens. Right?"

He nodded and held her gaze reassuringly. "Right."

It wouldn't be easy to have Brianne in their lives, and there was no way to avoid that if Jase wanted his daughter in his life. In the months since they'd found out about the pregnancy, they'd come to accept that that was how their life would be.

And that was one reason she loved him so much. How could she love a man who would renege on fatherhood or try to deny his responsibility? Jase, a big kid who liked to have fun and played a game for a living, had grown up fast. Or maybe the truth was, he'd always had that solid, responsible core beneath the fun-loving exterior.

"I guess we need to get rid of all these boxes," she said, looking around the kitchen. "And we should hit the grocery store and pick up a few things this afternoon."

"Okay."

A few hours later they were back in the kitchen, putting away the groceries they'd bought when the doorbell rang. They looked at each other.

Jase shrugged and straightened. "I'll get it."

He returned a moment later holding an envelope. When she saw his face, her abdomen tightened.

"I had to sign for it," he said.

"Is it the results of the DNA test?"

"Yeah."

She moved toward him, skirting an empty box still sitting on the floor. "Do you want me to open it?"

"No. I'll do it." He ripped it open and pulled it out. She watched his face. His lips parted as his eyes scanned the paper. Again. And again.

Her heart thudded and she dragged damp palms over her jeans.

CHAPTER THREE

Jase looked up at her. Said nothing.

"What is it?" Remi asked.

He gave his head a shake and looked back at the paper. "I'm not the father."

Remi's heart continued to pound as she stared at him and it was suddenly difficult to breathe. Not. Did he say *not*? "You're *not* the father?"

She reached for the paper and took it. He let go and rubbed his forehead.

She read the results and focused on the zero percent chance that Jase was the father of Brianne's baby.

Thank god. Oh thank god. Relief flowed through her, making her dizzy and a bit lightheaded. She wanted to laugh and jump up and down. Tears came to her eyes—tears of happiness.

Oh my god! She'd never dared hope this could really be the result! It was almost too good to believe. She let out a shaky breath and swiped at her eyes. Then she looked at Jason. "This is so good!"

He still stared into space, the corners of his mouth turned down, his eyes sad. "Good?"

Her heart went cold in her chest and her smile faded. "Aren't you happy?"

"I don't know. I don't know what I am." He pinched the bridge of his nose. "I think there might be a mistake."

She gaped at him. A mistake? Was he serious? These tests were apparently incredibly accurate. When he'd first found out about the pregnancy, he'd told Brianne there must be a mistake. Timing and pregnancy tests, those kinds of mistakes. But a DNA test? Jesus!

"It's not even a little equivocal," she ventured. "It says a zero per cent chance."

"I was sure I was the father." He blinked, his eyes unfocused.

Brianne had lied. She *had* slept with someone else. Remi's insides tightened. She watched Jason as he came to that realization.

"She screwed around on me."

"Not necessarily." She dropped the paper to the coffee table and moved closer, sliding her arms around his waist. "It probably happened after you broke up. The timing is never for sure."

"Yeah. Like the next day."

"Jase. You and I slept together the first night we met, which was only a week after you broke up with her. And you're the one who ended things."

He couldn't be jealous that Brianne had slept with another guy. Could he?

He removed her arms from his waist and stepped away. "I guess I'm just shocked," he said in a low voice. "I really believed her."

The way he distanced himself from her hurt. She gripped her fingers together, unsure what to say.

"I should call Brianne," he said. "She probably got the results too."

Remi'd gotten more used to Jase talking to his ex, but she still didn't like it. She wanted to be more secure, but it was hard, dammit, when Brianne had something so important to Jase. His baby.

But now she *didn't*, and relief swelled inside Remi that things would be done between Jase and Brianne forever now.

Curious about how Brianne was taking this and how she'd deal with it, and oh holy hell yeah, *who was the real father*, Remi said, "Yeah. Call her."

Jase pulled his cell phone out and pushed a button. "Hey," he said. "It's me. Did you—" He cleared his throat. "Did you get the DNA test results?" He listened, closing his eyes.

Remi studied his beautiful face, the square jaw with the chin dimple, his short dark brown hair still a bit mussed from her running her hands through it.

"Who is the father, Brianne?"

Remi's body tightened.

"I see. Great." His jaw tensed and his thick eyebrows drew down over his eyebrows. "I can't believe you did that."

Did what? Slept with another guy?

"I'm so fucking pissed off right now I can't even speak," he growled into the phone. "I want to—" He stopped, the hand now holding the phone curling into a fist. "Bye, Brianne."

Even though this was what Remi had really wanted deep down inside, the tension and anguish was almost unbearable. Nausea churned in her stomach and she had trouble swallowing through a tight throat.

Jase shook his head and looked at Remi. He knew she'd just asked a question, but he wasn't sure what it was. He just stared at her.

"What did she say?" she said again. "Did she know?"

"She was trying to say a lot," he bit out. "But I didn't want to listen to any more lies. For fuck's sake." He shoved a hand into his hair and turned away from Remi. Brianne had fucking lied to him, over and over, for the last six months. She'd told him there was no one else. Insisted he was the father. Insisted she still loved him. Christ, after he'd broken up with her, she'd kept calling and calling, trying to get back together. What the hell had that all been about? He looked at an empty cardboard box on the floor and gave it a kick, sending it flying across the room with a loud pop.

Remi jumped, her hand going to her chest. "Jesus, Jase."

"Fuck. I'm sorry, Remi." He rubbed his face. "I'm just so pissed off."

She bit her bottom lip and regarded him with somber eyes. "I see that."

The weird thing was, he wasn't sure what he was more pissed off about. The fact that Brianne had lied to him—or the fact that he wasn't actually a father.

He'd been to the hospital to see her the day she was born. He'd taken her a damn teddy bear with a big pink bow around its neck. He'd been to see her every day in the hospital. And she wasn't his daughter.

She was beautiful, with a perfect face and dark blue eyes and the prettiest little mouth. She was bright-eyed and alert, and when he'd seen her and held her warm, blanket-wrapped little body, he'd fallen in love with her.

And she wasn't his daughter.

He looked at Remi, staring back at him with shadowed eyes.

"Well," he said. "That's that, I guess."

He picked up the empty box and began to flatten it for recycling. "I'll get rid of these."

"Okay." She blinked and pushed another empty box toward him. "We're all done. Um. Are you going to call your parents?"

Fuck. Yeah, he'd have to do that. His mom was all thrilled that she was a grandmother, and now he had to tell her she wasn't. Another burst of hot anger at Brianne rushed through him. Dammit. Hadn't she realized how many people's lives she was impacting with that bullshit?

"Yeah. I'll have to call them. I'll do it tomorrow."

He'd helped Brianne pick out baby furniture for Emily's room in her condo, before Emily had arrived. They hadn't known Emily would be a girl, so Brianne had decorated it in yellow and white. He'd spent a fortune on the *Petit Trésor* crib Brianne had wanted. He didn't care about the money. That didn't matter. He'd planned to buy another one just like it to have here, for when Emily could start spending time away from her mother. The bedroom that had been Jasmine's was, in his mind, Emily's room.

"Jase?"

He looked up at Remi and realized he was standing there holding a cardboard box, staring into space.

"More coffee?"

"Oh. Sure. I'll have some."

She sighed and refilled his mug.

He'd known it wouldn't be easy to be a part-time father, on top of the fact that he travelled a lot, playing hockey. But Brianne had agreed that they would work out a custody arrangement that would take that into consideration. And he had Remi, who loved babies and children. He'd worked it all out in his mind, accepted that his life was going to change, and it would all be good.

He was looking forward to seeing his family at Christmas, but as they'd planned the trip to Winnipeg, he'd been hesitant to leave town because of the baby who would be there by then. And now she was here but it didn't matter, because she wasn't his.

"Jase?"

"Huh?" He looked at Remi.

"I said it's really starting to snow."

"Oh. Yeah." He glanced at the windows. "It is."

"You seem awfully…distracted. Do you want to talk about it?"

"Talk about what?"

"Emily. Brianne."

He caught the tightness at the corners of her eyes, the tension in her pretty mouth. Emily and Brianne had never been one of her favorite things to talk about. "Nah," he said. "I'm good. Want to go to IKEA today?"

She nodded, swallowed, but didn't say anything more.

As they shopped for new dishes and glasses and knives, his mind kept going over and over things, all those calls from Brianne telling him she loved him, insisting she hadn't slept with someone else, that he was the father. He'd eventually convinced her that they were *not* getting back together, because he was in love with Remi. She'd accepted that and he'd kept their contact to a minimum, just making sure she was looking after herself and therefore the baby. Later he'd gotten more involved, taking her to appointments and then helping her get the baby's room ready.

And later, as he and Remi ate dinner, he kept thinking about the doctor's appointments he taken Brianne to, the ultrasound appointment where they'd first seen the baby growing inside her. The baby he'd thought was his.

As they were getting ready for bed that night, he said, "Remi?"

"Mmm?"

"You should go off the Pill."

She blinked at him as she unzipped her jeans. "What?"

"I want a baby."

She kicked off the jeans, staring at him with heavy-lidded eyes, her heart-shaped face with its small chin so pretty. His gaze tracked down over her body in more sexy underwear.

"I want you to move in with me. I want you to marry me. I want to have a baby with you."

She gave her head a little shake. "Yeah. We will. Some day."

"I want it now."

"Sure, hon. We can talk about it tomorrow." She yawned. "I'm already half asleep."

He stripped off his sweatshirt and shucked his jeans and underwear and socks as Remi removed her sexy lingerie, climbed onto the big bed and burrowed beneath the covers.

He reached for her and pulled her into his arms. He was big

and she was small, but they fit together perfectly. He sought her mouth with his and took a long, slow kiss.

"Okay," he said. "We'll talk more tomorrow."

Jase had to get up to go to a morning practice again, and once more Remi stayed in bed a little longer, enjoying the luxury of sleeping in. He bent over to kiss her goodbye before he headed out and she gave him a sleepy smile.

"What are you going to do today?" he asked, brushing her hair off her face.

"Christmas shopping. And I have some marking that has to be done over the Christmas break."

"Are you shopping for me?"

Another smile tugged at her lips. "Maybe. Maybe I already have."

"You won't be able to pack that Ferrari in your suitcase and take it on the plane."

She laughed and snuggled deeper into the covers. "I'll have to return it then."

He laughed. "We're going to Rouge tonight with Dominic and Paula, and Matthieu and the new girl he's seeing, right? Do you want to go out for dinner before?"

"Mmm. Sure."

"I'll call you later."

"'Kay."

She sighed and closed her eyes again, drifting back to sleep as the house became silent. Then she remembered last night... *"You should go off the Pill..."* Her eyes popped open and she frowned. That was just crazy talk.

She flopped onto her back and stared at the ceiling, now wide awake. Jase hadn't reacted like she'd expected to the news that he wasn't the father of Brianne's baby. And then what the hell had that been…he wanted her to get pregnant?

She glanced at the clock. Ack! She had to get her butt in gear to meet Delise at the mall. She tossed aside the covers and hurried into the bathroom to shower. As the water heated up, she found her container of pills in her purse. She stared at it for a moment then punched one of the little tablets out and tossed it into her mouth.

She quickly showered, dressed, downed a cup of coffee then headed to the mall. After an exchange of text messages, she found Delise standing near Santa's Castle. Delise smiled and moved toward her, tossing her long auburn curls back over her shoulder.

"Look at this place." Delise waved a hand at the line-up of kids waiting to see Santa. "You could not pay me enough to work here."

Remi took in the kids, girls dressed up in frilly red dresses and boys in little vests. One baby screamed as her mother tried to set her on Santa's lap, her little round face red and scrunched up. Another little boy tried to climb the picket fence that kept the line-up from spilling into the mall, and when his mother hauled him down he howled too.

She grinned. "They're so cute."

"They're little monsters."

"Come on. We don't need to hang around here if it's stressing you out. Hey, and speaking of kids, I have news."

Delise stopped dead and turned to face her, eyes big behind the stylish rectangular frames of her glasses. "What? The DNA test?"

"Yes." Remi smiled.

Delise's mouth dropped. "Not Jason's?"

"Nope." She knew she was beaming, she couldn't help it. It was such a relief.

"Oh my god! That's incredible!" Delise grabbed her and they

hugged, swaying back and forth. "Oh, Rem, honey, I'm so happy for you!"

"Yeah, well, I'm happy for me too. But Jase isn't."

"What?" Delise drew back and looked at her with her forehead furrowed. "He's not happy about it?"

"He was really weird about it, actually."

"You know, maybe we should go for lunch."

"We just got here!"

"I know, but this conversation needs to be had sitting down, I think."

Remi laughed. "Okay, whatever. We have all afternoon to shop."

They went to a restaurant in the mall and managed to snag the last open table. Remi unwound her scarf from around her neck and hung her jacket on a nearby coat rack, then slid into the booth. She picked up the menu. "I am hungry," she said. "I've only had coffee this morning."

They ordered more coffee and sandwiches, and then Delise said, "Okay, tell me about the baby and Jase. If he's not the father, who is? That skinny bitch cheated on him, didn't she?"

Remi laughed. Delise could call Brianne a bitch, but she couldn't. She really didn't even know Brianne very well. She knew *of* her because of her modeling career. Her face and body were all over the city, advertising clothing stores and makeup and a big swimsuit line. She was tall and gorgeous, with big boobs and a killer body. Even pregnant, she'd only had small baby bump, and was probably already back to pre-pregnancy weight and ready to fulfill the big Victoria's Secret contract she'd landed just before she'd gotten pregnant. Or had she lost that contract? Remi wasn't sure, but she did know Jase hadn't been happy about the thought of Brianne and the baby moving to New York.

"I have no idea who the father is. Jase called her last night and I don't know what she said. He was furious, but I don't know if it was because she cheated on him before they broke up."

"Why would he care?" Delise asked, wrapping her hands around her cup of coffee.

"That's a good question," Remi said slowly. She poured a little milk into her coffee, picked up her spoon and stirred. "I was wondering that last night too. It…" She hesitated, her stomach going tight and achy again. "It made me wonder why he was so upset. And he wasn't saying much."

"Is he disappointed? Did he really want that baby?"

"Apparently he did. And now he wants *me* to have a baby."

Delise's mouth fell open. "Shut the front door. Really?"

"Well, that's what he said last night." She shook her head. "Maybe it was just a reactive comment."

Their sandwiches arrived. "This looks good," Remi said, picking up her grilled cheese sandwich and biting into it hungrily. Warm melty cheese and buttery crisp bread flooded her taste buds with yumminess.

"So he wants a baby?" Delise resumed their conversation. "What did else did he say?"

"He didn't want to talk much about it, but he was really distracted and…distant."

"He'd been pretty involved with things," Delise pointed out. "Taking Brianne to appointments and helping pick out things for the baby's room."

"I know." Remi wrinkled her nose. She hadn't exactly enjoyed the fact that Jase had spent so much time with Brianne, but after everything they'd been through, she trusted that he loved her and the only reason he was doing that was because he wanted to be there for his child. "I guess he'd accepted the fact that he was going to be a father, and now…he's not."

"But you must be relieved."

"Oh god, I am *so* relieved! I almost can't believe it! But then I kind of feel like a horrible person. How many times did I wish the baby wasn't his? But Jase was so sure of it I guess I'd accepted it too. And now…it feels awful to be so happy, when he's disappointed."

"Maybe it will just take him a little while to adjust." Delise smiled. "I know he's crazy about you."

Remi smiled back at her friend. "Thanks."

After lunch, they hit the stores. Remi knew exactly what she was buying for Jasmine and Kyle, but it was harder to know what to buy for Jase's family. She'd met them but she didn't know any of them that well, and what the heck did you buy millionaire hockey players, anyway? They could buy anything they wanted. Jase had been no help coming up with ideas. "Sex toys," he'd suggested. "For my brothers. I know they'd like that."

She'd rolled her eyes, but now she was thinking that might be the best thing she'd come up with. And hey, sex toys were really a present for their girlfriends too, right? Except she didn't think Matt had a girlfriend. Logan was bringing his new girlfriend Nicole home for Christmas to meet everyone. Tag and Kyla would be there. But they could not be opening gifts of sex toys in front of Jase's parents on Christmas morning.

"Hey!" she said to Delise. "I can buy Tag and Kyla that Master Edition Trivial Pursuit game. We had fun playing that at the lake last summer. Then Kyla and I can kick their butts again."

Delise laughed. "Sounds good."

"Oh wait! I should buy them things from Chicago."

"Garrett popcorn."

"Yes! But I can't buy that until we're leaving."

"What about deep-dish pizza?"

Remi frowned. "How would I do that? I can't see packing a pizza in my suitcase."

"I know a place that ships."

"But probably not to Canada."

"Ugh. Probably not."

"But I make a pretty good deep-dish pizza… I wonder if I could take over Mrs. Heller's kitchen and make pizzas one night."

"She might already have meals planned. On the other hand, she might like having someone else do the cooking."

Remi tapped her chin. "I could check with her ahead of time. Not tell her what I'm making, of course. And I could buy deep-dish pizza pans and leave them with her."

Now with some ideas, they continued shopping. Remi helped Delise pick out some things from Sephora for her sisters and her mom, and an iPod for her father. "He says he wants one," Delise said with a shrug.

"The only one left is Jase," Remi finally said, loaded down with shopping bags.

"A baby," Delise said. "A baby for Christmas."

Remi stared at her.

"I'm kidding!"

Remi shook her head. "Not funny."

"How about some sexy lingerie?"

"Oh, good idea! He likes dressing up in a garter belt and stockings."

Delise choked on her laughter. "Omigod, just picturing him dressed like that is hysterical."

Remi knew Delise had meant lingerie for her. "I have enough sexy lingerie. But getting back to the sex toy idea...hmmm. Maybe I'll have to do some online shopping. But I'll need something else I can give him that he can open in front of his family."

"Just imagine him pulling out a set of handcuffs on Christmas morning."

Now it was Remi's turn to laugh. But she had an idea for the Christmas morning gift...

CHAPTER FOUR

Jase had been planning to do Christmas shopping too after practice, but then he remembered he'd been planning to buy Emily Christmas presents and now he didn't have to. Well, he could, but that would be weird. Wouldn't it?

He sighed and sat on a stool at the beautiful new island in the kitchen. The house was quiet and empty. Really empty without Remi there. Because she belonged there. Dammit.

He had some phone calls to make. His parents. His brothers. Yeah, really looking forward to that. He picked up his cell phone. His gut tightened.

His mom was home. He made a little small talk then said, "We got the results of the paternity test."

"I wondered if that's why you're calling."

"Yeah. So. It turns out the baby's not mine."

The phone was so silent against his ear he wondered if his mom had hung up.

"You still there, Mom?"

"Yes." Her voice had gone soft. "I'm here. How do you feel about that?"

"Confused." He rubbed his forehead. "I was so sure…"

"I know. Are you happy, though?"

"No." He scowled. "Remi thinks I should be, but I can't say I actually feel happy about this."

"You're disappointed."

"I guess I am. I just had it all straight in my head and then… well. Remi doesn't get it."

He heard his mom's soft sigh. "Well, I get it. Because I'm kind of disappointed too."

He swallowed. "I knew you would be. I'm sorry, Mom."

"You don't need to apologize. This wasn't your doing. Although I hope you learned an important lesson about safe sex."

"Jeez, Mom."

"Is that why Brianne didn't want me to come and help with the baby? Because she knew?"

"I'm not sure. She says she really thought I was the father, but then she obviously lied about the fact that there wasn't anyone else, so who knows." Bitterness edged his voice.

"I'm sure Remi is relieved," Mom said.

"Yup." His mouth twisted.

They talked for a little longer, planning for Christmas when the family would be all together. Then he called his brothers to give them the same story. He got hold of Logan in Minneapolis.

"You don't need to say 'I told you so,'" he said to Logan.

"Oh hell yeah, I do," Logan said. "Jesus, Jase. Thank god you got that test done! Can you imagine if you hadn't? If you'd—"

"I got it done," Jase said through clenched teeth. "Let it go."

He'd been prepared for a lecture from his brother after the way he and Tag had bugged him last summer about having the paternity test done. His insides burned as he remembered how strongly he'd asserted his confidence in the fact that he was the father. How he'd been sure Brianne had been honest with him. How he'd gotten his mother all excited to be a grandmother.

"I was a fucking idiot," he said. "I'll admit it. I'm kicking myself in the ass about it. Mom's all disappointed and I feel like I let her down in some weird twisted way."

"You're not an idiot," Logan said. He gave a heavy sigh. "Look, it's all worked out for the best, right?"

Jason shook his head. Another person who thought this was a great outcome. Just. Fucking. Great. "Yeah," he said shortly. "I'm ecstatic. Gotta go. I have to call Tag and Matt."

He hung up and called Tag's cell phone number. No answer, so he called Kyla's cell phone and ended up talking to her. She kept her own thoughts to herself, more than Logan, which Jase appreciated very much at that moment, and promised to tell Tag and have him call him back later. When Jase called Matt, he ended up leaving a voice mail.

He was sick of talking about it.

His mind replayed his short conversation with Brianne yesterday and he gritted his teeth. He'd cut her off before she could tell him any more lies. But they needed to talk. He needed answers to the questions backing up in his brain. He needed to put an end to this once and for all.

He grabbed his keys and his jacket. He was going to get answers.

It took him less than half an hour to get to Brianne's condo. She seemed surprised to hear him, but buzzed him in and he rode up the elevator with his guts in a snarl.

She opened the door to him alone, standing there tall and slender, wearing black yoga pants and a T-shirt. She didn't look as if she'd just had a baby, although the T-shirt was loose. But weirdly, the T-shirt had a stain on it and she wore no makeup. Her hair was falling out of a ponytail, lank strands hanging around her face, and dark circles beneath her eyes gave her a tired look. Whoa. This was *not* like her. The first couple of times he'd visited when she'd brought Emily home, he didn't think she'd looked so tired.

"Hey," he said. "We need to talk."

Her full lips pressed together but she nodded. "Sure."

"Where's Emily?"

"Sleeping, thank god. I just put her down in the crib. She was up all night screaming, then she slept for a few hours this morning, and I just managed to get her back to sleep again. Then I had to do some laundry."

"Is she okay?" He frowned. "Why was she screaming?"

"I don't know!" She took a breath. "Sorry. I'm tired. I don't know why she was crying. I changed her diaper, I fed her, I burped her. All I could do was walk around carrying her all night. God, it's frustrating."

Jason chewed on his bottom lip. "I'm no help, I guess. I don't know much about babies either."

"I read the book and—oh. Come in. Have a seat. We may only have a little while until she wakes up again."

He wanted to see Emily. But then again, he didn't. He sat on one end of Brianne's leather couch and she sat at the other end.

"I read the book," she said again. "Apparently sometimes they just do that and nobody really knows why."

"Colic?"

"Yes, maybe. Over-stimulated, maybe." She leaned her head back against the couch and blew out a breath. "I've been reading stuff to try to learn what I need to do."

That was good. "Did your mom go home?"

"Yes. She stayed for a week. She says she'll come back if I need her. But..."

"But what?"

"I felt like she was taking over." Brianne shot him a quick, wary look. "She was here to help and I appreciated it, but she wanted to look after the baby and...well, *I* want to look after Emily. I feel like she won't love me if I don't look after her, so I didn't want my mom doing it all."

Jason blinked and gazed at Brianne. Wow. "It sounds like you really love her."

"Who? Emily? Or my mom?"

His lips quirked. "Well, both. But Emily, I meant."

She turned her head where it leaned against the couch cushions and met his gaze. "Of course I love her." A wrinkle appeared between her eyebrows. "Why would that surprise you?"

"Uh…" Because she hadn't planned to have a baby. Because having a baby had interfered with her modeling career. Because she'd been more worried about not gaining weight than the health of their…uh, *her* baby. "I'm not. Do you…do you have anyone else that can help? You need to get sleep too." Fuck. He was not going to offer to help. Emily wasn't his baby. But still… she was a baby, a helpless little baby…*no*. She wasn't his responsibility anymore and neither was Brianne, that was for damn sure.

"Yes. Don't worry about me." Her mouth twisted a little.

He nodded. "Maybe you could pay someone to come help. Like a nanny." He knew she wasn't hurting for money. He could afford to pay someone…but again, he had to remind himself it wasn't his responsibility.

"I guess I could. I'd have no idea how to find someone. And besides…that would be kind of like my mom here, doing everything. *I* want to look after her."

"Yeah. Okay."

A moment of silence expanded between them. Then she said, "I'm sorry, Jase." She rubbed her forehead. "I really did think you were the father. That wasn't a lie."

His jaw tightened. "But there *was* someone else. And you knew that all along. You should have told me that at the beginning."

"It was one time. And it was after we broke up. I was still in love with you. I thought we could get back together." Her voice hitched a little. "I couldn't tell you that I'd slept with someone else if I wanted you to take me back."

"Yes." His teeth ground together a little. "You could have. You should have. You should have been honest. You let me go all these months believing I was going to be a father, buying stuff for the baby, going for frickin' ultrasound appointments with you, helping you with her room. Christ." His eyes burned and he dragged a hand across them. "And now I find out the truth, I feel like something's been taken away from me. Except…" He swallowed. "She was never mine."

"I'm sorry," she whispered. "Yes, I did want us to get back together. I wanted that so much. That one night with…well, it wasn't important. I really was sure it was you who was the father. I *wanted* it to be you who was the father."

"Wishful thinking doesn't make it so."

"I know. I know!"

"So if it was one time, you do know who the real father is then." He gave her a narrow-eyed look. "Yesterday on the phone you started to tell me you didn't know. What's the truth, Brianne? I don't even know whether to believe anything you say."

She dropped her gaze. "That's the truth. It was one time. I do know who the father is."

"Have you told him?"

"No. I just found out yesterday," she reminded him.

"But you are going to."

"Yes!"

Jesus, that poor guy was in for a shock. Jase debated asking who it was. Nah. He didn't really want to know. He was done.

He studied Brianne. Had she really believed he was the father?

He'd been in love with her once. It seemed like a long, long time ago. And now, he wondered why.

He cast a glance toward the bedroom where Emily was sleeping and an aching knot formed in his chest. Fuck. Then he looked at Brianne, seeing again how wiped out and stressed she looked. He was a stupid idiot, but… "If you need anything, you can call me," he said gruffly. "I mean if you need anything for Emily. If you need help…time to rest. If her real father doesn't…"

He cleared his throat. "If he doesn't want to be involved and you need…well. Let me know."

Brianne's eyes filled with sadness and her mouth trembled. "Jase."

He shook his head and rose to his feet. "I have to go."

Fuck. Was Brianne still having crazy ideas about them getting back together? He had to get out of there. He didn't want to give her the wrong idea by going there, or by making that stupid offer of help, except dammit, Emily was just a baby and he'd held her and thought she was his and…

Fuck.

Remi was sitting at her computer looking at wrist and ankle restraints that Velcroed to the bed sheets when Jason arrived at her apartment. He had a key and didn't use the security system, so the only warning she had that he'd arrived was the sound of the key in the lock and the door opening. She quickly closed the website. But she smiled. Those restraints were pretty cool. Jase'd probably like them. And so would she…

She turned to greet him, ready to ask about his day, his morning practice, where were they going for dinner and oh yeah, let's talk about having a baby. But he looked…what? Sad? Tired?

Her stomach clenched and she rose from the chair at the desk in her small living room. "Hey. How are you?" She went to him and wound her arms around his neck and hugged him, pressing her lips to the side of his neck. She breathed in his singular scent, warm athletic male and spicy shower gel.

"I'm okay." He set his hands on her waist and pulled her against him briefly, then set her away from him. She blinked. "You look nice," he said.

"Thanks." She glanced down at herself in her black strapless tube dress and black patent heels. She was all ready for their night out. "You look nice too." She took in his narrow black dress pants, the thin, grey V-neck sweater over a darker grey T-shirt, all topped with his soft, black leather jacket. "Did you make a reservation for dinner?"

"Yeah. At Mezzaluna."

She smiled. She liked the little Italian *trattoria*, and it wasn't far from Rouge, the club where they were meeting their friends. "Sounds good. I'm ready to go."

"Let's take a cab tonight."

"Sure."

Remi slipped on a silver knit cardigan then grabbed the silver trench coat she'd now worn a surprising number of times. The day Delise had convinced her to splurge on something so impractical had been the day she'd urged Remi to go out and start having fun. And the day she'd met Jase. She wrapped a big, navy blue pashmina around her throat, and picked up gloves and a small purse into which she'd transferred cell phone, lipstick, a credit card and a little money.

Jase was quiet in the cab but that was okay. They didn't need to have a big personal conversation with the taxi driver as an audience. But once inside the restaurant at their table for two, small lamps casting a mellow glow and jazz music playing softly around them, she met his eyes. "We have to talk, Jase."

"I know." He looked at his menu. "Antipasti? I like the seafood."

She bit her lip. "Sure. I like that too."

"And wine," he said. "Let's get that Pinot Grigio you like."

Dining in restaurants like Mezzaluna was still new to Remi. Expensive wines and elegant dishes were not something she'd grown up with. Even when her parents had been alive, they'd been busy doctors who spent a lot of time in Africa providing medical care, not eating in exclusive downtown restaurants with their three kids.

She swallowed a sigh. Obviously even though he agreed they had to talk, he was putting it off.

When they had glasses of golden wine in front of them, he said, "How was your shopping?"

"Pretty good. I'm almost done." She told him her ideas for his family.

"Great." He nodded, but she wasn't sure he'd even heard what she said, his attention seemingly somewhere else. She'd seen this before. Jase managed his ADHD well as an adult, but sometimes wandering attention or zoning out during a conversation happened. She reached for his hand and covered it with hers on the table.

"Hey," she said softly. "Look at me."

He met her eyes then gave a small grimace. "Sorry, Rem. I'm here."

She squeezed his hand a bit and he turned his over and wrapped his big strong fingers around hers. "I know. Come on. Let's do this now." She searched his face. "I'm relieved that the baby's not yours. I thought you would be too."

"How can you say that?" he asked slowly. "How could you think I'd be happy about that?"

"Jase. Remember when you found out Brianne was pregnant? You lost your mind. You thought you got a girl pregnant by accident. You'd already broken up with her and you know what a nightmare it was going to be, having her in our lives, forever. You knew how much it was going to hurt me, even though it happened before we met. You were so pissed off and horrified when you found out about it, you went out and got drunk and got arrested. And now you *want* that?"

"She wouldn't have been in our lives forever," he muttered.

Remi sighed. "You know what I mean. If you really were the father, and Emily really was your daughter…"

He flinched as if she'd punched him.

"You and Brianne would have been joined by that for the rest of your lives. Aren't you *happy* that's not the case?"

He gazed back at her. "I guess. Yeah."

"You *guess?*"

His eyes shadowed and he nodded. "I'm not sure what to say, Rem. I don't love Brianne. Having to continue some kind of weird relationship as parents didn't really seem that huge of a problem to me. Once Brianne accepted that that was *all* our relationship would be, and once you'd accepted it, it wasn't that big of a deal. But…" He paused. "I do care about Emily."

"You know how hard it was for me."

He frowned. "I know. But we worked it out, and we both agreed. We love each other and we'd be okay."

"Yes, but…" She made a little sound, almost like a little growl. "I don't think you understand."

"No. I don't. And I don't think you're understanding how *I'm* feeling."

"I'm trying to. Break it down for me."

He looked down at the table and she waited not so patiently. "I feel like I've lost something, Rem," he finally said slowly. "I know Emily wasn't ever really mine, but I feel like I lost her. It sucks."

She bit her lip, her heart aching for him, and nodded again. She got that. "I'm sorry, Jase." She squeezed his hand tighter, and they sat there silently for another moment. Then she asked, "Why'd you say that last night? That you want to have a baby."

He frowned. "Because I do."

"You were serious?"

"Yeah."

"Oh my god." She stared at him. "Are you *that* disappointed? You really want a baby?"

"Yeah."

She stared at him. "That makes me feel like all you want me for is to procreate with."

"Christ no!" His eyebrows flew up. "That's not true. I told you before, Remi. I wished it had been *you* who'd been pregnant. I want to have a baby with *you*."

"But I'm not ready for a baby right now."

"When, then?"

"Well for one thing, I'd like to be married first."

"We can get married tomorrow."

She laughed, even though that sort of made her sad. "No, we can't."

"Okay, next week."

"Jase. I don't want to get married like that. I don't need a great big formal wedding, but I'd like to plan a few things, and our wedding day should be special on its own, because we want to get married, not just something to get out of the way so we can have a baby. And even if we get married, this isn't the right time for me. You know that. You know I'm trying to have a life for myself."

"I know." He groaned and took a big gulp of his wine. "I know, Remi. But damn, I'm just so bummed about this whole thing."

"I can see that."

They looked at each other across the small table. This wasn't going very well. "Could we just maybe talk about it a bit more? Having a child is a big decision. Just give me some time, Jase."

"How much time?"

"I don't know. Maybe…a year?"

"I thought maybe a few days. Or a week." But his lips quirked. He nodded slowly. "Okay. We can talk about it. And you can think about it more."

She let out a big, long breath. Some of that tension eased a bit and she relaxed back into her chair. "Okay. Thank you." She flashed him a smile. Then she asked, "Did you call your family?"

"Yeah. I didn't talk to Tag or Matt. I left a message with Kyla and a voice mail for Matt."

"Your mom?"

He nodded and looked down at his wine. "Yep."

She could imagine how hard that was for him. How many times had he told them the paternity test wasn't necessary? And now this.

She hated that he was unhappy. *Hated* it. And she hated Brianne for doing this to him. She so wanted to make him feel better, she'd do anything for him. Well, almost anything. Have a baby…?

Except…except…how many times had she thought how much she *wanted* to have Jase's baby since she'd found out about Brianne's pregnancy? How she too had wanted it to be her who'd gotten pregnant.

She pushed those thoughts away and tried to enjoy their dinner.

As Jason ate his grilled veal chop with faro and cippolini onions, and she the spicy Tuscan seafood stew, they talked about their Christmas plans, the few days they'd spend in Winnipeg. Jase looked happier when he talked about going home and seeing his family, talking about how he wanted to go to the community center near his home and skate like he had when he was a kid.

After dinner, they met Jase's teammates Dominic and Matthieu, and Dominic's wife and Matthieu's new girlfriend at Rouge, a trendy bar full of beautiful people.

"This is where Jase and I met," Remi told the group as they sipped martinis and scotch and imported beers.

"I remember that," Dominic said with a grin and a wink. "You two hit it off pretty quick. I seem to recall you leaving together that night."

Remi tried not to blush. Picking up guys in bars was so not her thing. "Hey, it turned out pretty good," she said, her cheeks warm.

Jase brushed her hair back and gave her a hot look. "I thought you weren't my type. Look how wrong I was."

"Aaaaaw." The chorus of mocking approval from the other players made both Remi and Jase laugh.

They danced and drank and talked and laughed. At one point, Remi sat on his lap with her arm around his neck while he talked to Matthieu and Dominic. When Matthieu got up to go get another drink, she nuzzled Jase's ear and kissed his cheek. "Mmm. You smell good." She loved the warm, male scent of his skin.

His hand tightened on her hip and he turned his mouth in to hers for a long, soft kiss. "Having fun?"

"Yeah. You?" She rubbed her nose on his jaw.

"Yeah. Let's go home."

She smiled. "Already?"

"Mmm. Wanna take you to bed." He kissed her cheek, his breath warm, his body hard against hers. A thrill of lust zinged through her.

"We should stay a little longer," she protested, her eyelids dropping slowly closed as he continued to nuzzle and kiss her.

"Why?"

"I don't know…" She let out a sigh. "Okay. Let's go."

They took a cab home. Sitting in the back seat, Jase turned to her to kiss her again, laying his hand on her bare knee then sliding it higher, up under her dress. Her girl parts gave a warm squeeze as lust pooled there. Heat gathered beneath her clothes, spreading over her skin. Jase moved his mouth on hers, kissing her, kissing her again, and again, his tongue sliding into her mouth to taste her. She moaned.

His fingers played higher, daringly, dangerously higher on her thighs. "Jase," she whimpered. "Stop…"

"Nuh." He found her panties and stroked over them. She kept her thighs closed despite the instinctive way they wanted to part to allow him access to where she ached with need.

"Not here…"

He brushed his bristly jaw against hers and she dragged her

eyes open to watch the lights of the city paint him with gold, then red, then shadows again as they turned onto Lakeshore Drive. With his face so close to her, she admired the shape of his nose and his smooth cheekbones, his eyelids heavy with lust, his beautiful mouth parted. His big shoulders blocked her view out the window and more heat mainlined through her veins as he dragged his tongue along the sensitive side of her neck.

She lifted a languid hand to his shoulder and dug her fingers into his jacket, the leather soft as cream.

"Love you, Remi."

"Love you too."

His fingers continued their wicked exploration, and with a soft sigh of surrender, she opened her thighs to his touch because she needed it so badly, the ache there now ravenous, and she slid into a haze of passion, oblivious to the taxi driver sitting in front of them as Jase kissed her again and again and his fingers stroked over her panties.

Awareness returned moments later when the cab stopped in front of the house, and she blinked as Jase slowly drew away, reaching for his wallet. She licked her lips and dragged air into her lungs, tugging her dress down on her thighs before alighting from the car.

The snap of the cold night air outside the warm car cleared the gauzy sexual longing that surrounded her, and as Jase paid the taxi driver, she hastened up to the front door and entered the code into the new entry system Jase had installed. He entered right behind her and closed the door, then scooped her up in his arms and headed for the stairs.

"Jase!" She grabbed on to him, still wearing coat and gloves. His smile gleamed white in the dim house as he climbed the stairs.

"You know I love those shoes," he murmured. "Gonna get you out of your coat. Maybe the dress…it's pretty sexy too. Maybe we'll leave it on…"

He lowered her to the floor in the bedroom, her feet still wearing the spiky black shoes, and she tossed her little purse onto an armchair as he clicked on the lamp. Then he reached for the belt and buttons of her shiny trench coat. He pushed it off her shoulders, his hands lingering there. "You have the prettiest shoulders," he murmured, and bent to kiss one. His mouth opened and lingered there and her eyes once again drifted closed as her knees dissolved. He drew his tongue along her collarbone and kissed the other shoulder, his whiskers excitingly masculine against her flesh, the wet fire of his mouth filling her up with hot sparks.

At the back of her mind, she was dimly relieved that he was back to being himself, that he seemed to have gotten over the news he'd received yesterday. Last night he'd been so silent and broody and she'd been worried about what he'd been thinking and feeling. Now his usual insatiable sexual appetite for her had returned and reassured her of his feelings for her.

He gently pushed her to sit on the side of the bed as he stripped his clothes off, and she watched with the pleasure she always felt at seeing him, his body so perfect, every muscle defined, his shoulders, his abs, his big thighs. Her gaze centered on his groin, the dense brown curls, his erection thick, his testicles big and heavy.

He stepped in front of her and she reached for him, desperate to touch him, to take the heavy weight of his cock in her hands, to feel the soft skin with her fingers. Her mouth hungering to taste him, she bent her head.

"Oh yeah," he groaned, planting his feet a little farther apart on the rug, his thigh muscles tensing. His hands came to her shoulders again, then stroked up the sides of her neck until he gently held her head. She opened her mouth over him, taking the smooth head inside, and erotic bliss slid through her veins. She hummed her delight, dragged her tongue around his shaft, getting him wet so she could take him deeper, and then deeper still. He tasted so good, warm and male, like sex and surrender, offering and acceptance. She cupped his balls, tested the weight of them, gently squeezed their firmness as her lips moved up and down on his cock and her tongue swirled around it.

His fingers tightened in her hair and his abs flexed and rippled. "Remi," he gasped. "That's so good. Gotta...gotta stop though..."

"Mmm." She lifted her gaze to meet his and gave her head a little negative shake. She loved this, loved doing this for him, loved the taste of him, the feel of him on her tongue.

"Yeah. Yeah...I'm close..."

She released him long enough to say "It's okay," then resumed her hungry sucking, her hand at the base of his shaft pumping too.

With firmer hands he pulled her head away. "No," he said. "Don't wanna come in your mouth tonight. Wanna come inside you."

"Oh." She couldn't really be disappointed in that, although she did love when he came in her mouth, relishing the exciting male taste of him in her throat. Her body suffused with heat and desire, she let him push her to her back on the bed and shove her dress up on her thighs. He lifted one leg to admire her shoes. He did have a bit of a fetish for high-heeled shoes and boots, and she had to admit she'd kind of gotten into that whole fantasy, finding herself feeling unspeakably wicked and sexy in bed sometimes wearing nothing but stiletto heels. She licked her lips as he kissed one ankle then the other, then folded her legs back, opening her to him, and more waves of heat cascaded over her.

Her pussy ached with need, and she hoped he would lean in and kiss her there. Her hips lifted a little in invitation. He shifted her on the bed and moved over her, so solid and radiating heat off his satiny skin. His weight on his arms, he lowered his head to kiss her. Another moan climbed in her throat at the silken feel of his tongue in her mouth.

"Wanna make a baby," he murmured against her cheek. "Now."

She blinked as his words penetrated the fog of heat and lust that enveloped them. "Jase."

"I want you to go off the Pill," he said, as he had last night. "I want a baby with you, Remi." His cheek rubbed hers.

She went very still against him.

CHAPTER FIVE

Remi gave a little push on his chest. "Jase."

"Remi…" He wanted her so bad, his cock huge and throbbing, his balls aching. He couldn't stop now—

"No. Wait."

She pushed at him again, harder. He opened his eyes and looked at her. Her eyebrows had pinched together and her mouth tightened.

" C'mon, Rem, I need you—"

"You need me? Or you need a baby?"

A long groan escaped him and he rolled away from her onto his back. "You. I need you. But yeah, I want a baby."

After a long moment dense with frustration and disquiet, she said quietly, "You said you'd give me time. And I meant more than a few hours."

"Yeah. I'm sorry. That just slipped out."

"Jase. You're scaring me," she whispered.

He frowned. "Scaring you? How?"

She sat up, tugging her dress down on her legs. A gust of wind hurled snow at the bedroom window."I-I feel like maybe you *wanted* to continue some kind of relationship with Brianne."

His mouth dropped open. "What are you saying? You think I still have feelings for her? That's crazy! How could you think that?"

"Because you're so broken up about the fact that this baby isn't yours and you're desperate to have another one."

He shook his head, trying to make sense of what she was saying. "That has nothing to do with Brianne. You're not making any sense."

She lifted her eyebrows then narrowed her eyes. "Great. I'm not making sense. Thank you very much." She pushed herself off the bed. The lamplight gleamed off her tangle of blonde hair and the smooth curve of her bare shoulders in the strapless dress. "I want to go back to my place tonight."

"Oh, come on, Rem…don't do this."

She shook her head, picking up her coat from the floor.

"I'm not—fuck." He dropped back onto the bed and stared at the ceiling. "Fuck."

She shoved her arms into the sleeves of the coat.

"Remi. It's snowing out. I've been drinking. I'm not taking you home."

"I'll call a cab."

"Don't. Come on. Come to bed. I promise I won't touch you." Bitterness edged his voice, his aching hard-on deflating somewhat.

Her heavy sigh reached his ears. "Jase. I can't get pregnant tonight, no matter how hard you try."

He looked up and saw the curve of her lips, and as their eyes met, he reluctantly smiled too. And then they both started laughing. Shit. He was acting like an idiot.

"Really?" he asked. "You mean my swimmers aren't so all-powerful that they can overcome your birth control? I'm not Super Virile Man?"

Remi smirked. "Just because you have a big cock doesn't mean your sperm are all-powerful."

"What? Seriously?"

She laughed. "Oh, honey. Don't tell me this is all about proving your virility."

"Nah. I can honestly say I've never been worried about that." Some guys got all puffed up about being able to knock a chick up; he hadn't felt that way when Brianne was pregnant. But damn, he *would* like to make Remi pregnant.

"I'll stay," she said with a wry smile. He watched her take off her coat and lay it over the arm of the chair then disappear into the bathroom.

But damn. Shit. Fuck. Everything had been going along fine, great, fantastic. He and Remi were solid, he was nuts about her, the baby had arrived healthy and perfect. But now, after getting the results of that damn DNA test, it felt as if everything was falling apart.

～

Over the next days, the topic of having a baby came up between them more often than Remi would have liked. Jase wasn't letting it go. She tried to not to let it bug her, but it was beginning to feel…uncomfortable. Oppressive. Annoying. Maybe it bothered her more because she was so conflicted about it herself. Because it was something she wanted so much—and yet didn't want.

How many times had she thought how much she wanted to have Jase's baby since she'd found out about Brianne's pregnancy? How she'd wanted it to be her who'd gotten pregnant.

Jase wasn't a big, dumb jock. He was a man—honorable, responsible, smart and funny. She knew he would make a good father. He was the man she wanted to spend the rest of her life with. So why was she being so difficult about this? Wouldn't it be easier to just agree to it?

And Jase still seemed sad and distracted. Not all the time. He was getting over the feeling that he'd lost something, but she could tell he wasn't himself yet. It was making her careful of what she said to him, how she chose her words, and made her sidestep any mention about babies and children and the future. She hated seeing him unhappy. And she hated this tension between them.

She talked to Delise on the phone.

"I still don't know what to get Jase for Christmas," she said. "He's impossible."

"I told you before—a baby."

"Oh. My. God." Remi rubbed her forehead. "Don't even joke about that. He's making me nucking futs. Apparently when he said he wanted to have a baby that night, he was serious."

"Oh. Oh wow."

"Yeah."

"Are you going to?"

Remi pursed her lips. "No."

"Really?"

"Not right now." She sighed. "We talked about this, remember? I've just started really living free and on my own. Making my own decisions, even if it is just to stay late at work, or have popcorn for dinner. And travelling. We took that trip to Europe when school ended last year. I've always wanted to travel and see the world, but there was never enough money left over when I was raising two teenagers, or the opportunity. I want to do more of that."

"You can travel with a baby."

Remi gave a delicate snort.

"Okay, it wouldn't be the same. I know what you're saying, Rem. But I know you do want kids."

"Yeah. I do." She smiled wistfully. "Some day. And I want them with Jase. I love him, Delise. I want to have a baby with him. I'm so torn about this. I've always wanted to be a mother. I mothered Jasmine and Kyle after my parents died. But when they grew up and moved on with their lives, I realized my whole life had been so wrapped up in them, I didn't have much of a life of my own."

"I know."

Yeah, Delise had been the one who'd encouraged her to start having fun and enjoying her freedom.

"I don't want that to happen with Jase. I love him, but I don't want to just be Jason Heller's girlfriend. I know how easy that would be to happen, not only because I love him and want to be with him all the time, but because he's rich and famous and talented. I want to be my own person."

"I know you do."

"I love him, but I'm mad at him too. It's so unfair of him, to want me to do that now. Just when I'm getting used to a taste of freedom."

"And you're not even married. He does plan to marry you, doesn't he?"

"Yes. He said we could get married tomorrow. And he wants me to move in with him. What should I do, Delise?"

"Well, maybe some nice aftershave…"

Remi couldn't help but laugh. "I mean about the whole baby thing."

"Oh. That." Delise's voice softened. "I can't tell you whether or not to have a baby."

"No, I'm not having a baby right now. But what do I do about Jase?"

"You give him time to get over grieving for the baby he never really had, while he gives you time to think about having a baby. Take your time, figure out what you really want, and then talk to him about it. I don't know anything about this stuff, but I know you two love each other. I know he cares about you, Remi, don't ever doubt that."

"You're such a good friend."

"I know."

Remi grinned.

~

Two days before they were to leave for Winnipeg, Jase was at her apartment helping her decide what to pack. The last game before the Christmas break was tomorrow night when the Wolves played the Rockies, and Remi would go watch with the other wives and girlfriends. The team treated them so well, something that had surprised her since she and Jase had only started seeing each other near the end of last season. She wanted to go watch the game and have fun with the other women and watch Jase win, and then the next morning they'd be off to Winnipeg and Jase would be too busy to think about babies.

Jase ordered pizza and opened a bottle of wine while she debated over the appropriate clothing.

"Church?" she called to him from her bedroom. "We're going to church?"

"Yes."

"Anything else special I need to know about? Fancy parties?"

He appeared in the doorway, filling it with his broad shoulders. "No, nothing fancy. Bring warm clothes for when we go skating."

"And skates?" He'd bought her a pair but she'd only worn them once.

"Do you have room in your suitcase?"

"I think so."

"If you don't, we'll borrow a pair for you there." His forehead creased. "Maybe from Kyla. I think my mom's feet are bigger than yours. Kyla's probably are too." Then he grinned. "We can borrow a kid's pair for you."

"Very funny." But she smiled as she folded a pair of black leggings.

They set the pizza on the coffee table in her living room, and with her favorite Christmas CD playing jazzy versions of Christmas songs, they sat on the couch to eat. She'd decorated a small tree in the corner with the ornaments she'd brought with her from the house and tiny white lights twinkling among the branches. With a glass of wine and pepperoni pizza and Jase there with her, a feeling of happiness expanded and spread inside her.

"So," he said. "Have you been thinking about it?"

Her smile disappeared and she sighed. "If you mean what I think you mean, how could I not, when you keep reminding me every hour."

He frowned. "You make it sound like I'm harassing you."

"Jase! You are!"

"No, I'm not. You said we could talk about it and you'd think about it. This is me asking if you've been thinking about it. That's all."

That tension inside her began to build again.

"I've told you. This isn't the right time in my life to have a baby."

"But there's no good reason for that," he insisted. "You admit you want kids. You love babies and you've always wanted your own. So why not?"

She sipped her wine, her throat aching a little. "I can't get pregnant right now to give you what you want," she whispered. "I just can't. And it's selfish of you to think I should."

"Selfish?" He gaped at her. "*I'm* selfish? You're the one who wants to be all free and independent and not tied down with anything." He tossed his half-eaten piece of pizza back into the box and rose to his feet. "Even me, apparently."

She watched open mouthed as he grabbed his jacket. "Where are you going?"

"I don't know. Home."

"But, Jase…" She stood too, clutching her wineglass. "Wait. Don't just walk out."

But he did. He walked out of her apartment without even another glance at her, closing the door firmly behind him.

A sharp pain stabbed through her chest and pressure rose up

into her face, hot and hard, making her eyes burn. She blinked rapidly and tried to swallow.

How could this be happening? When they'd opened that letter and read those results, she'd thought this nightmare was finally coming to an end. Done. Finished. She and Jase could move on with their lives together without that huge burden of him having a child with someone else, sharing custody, working around his travel schedule, having to deal with gorgeous supermodel Brianne Haskett in their lives.

It should have been wonderful and liberating… But things hadn't been this bad between them since they'd found out about Brianne's pregnancy just over six months ago.

Remembering that horrible time, when Jase had ended things between them, made her heart hurt so bad she almost couldn't breathe, and she dropped down to the couch. With unsteady hands she set the glass of wine on the table and tried to take a deep breath. Was it happening again? Really?

Last time she'd gone to him. She'd fought for him. For *them*. Although in the end, she hadn't had to fight very hard because Jase had really wanted them to be together too. But now…she was just confused. And hurt.

She debated her options. Call him? Right now? Later? Tomorrow? Try again to talk to him? Or let him work things out for himself? And hope that he did, and that he'd come back.

This couldn't be a break up. It couldn't be. After all they'd been through. She knew he loved her. She loved him. That had to mean something. That had to mean they could get through this, whatever "this" was. Maybe he just needed some time, to get over the disappointment and to realize this was all for the best.

Jase got into his SUV parked on the snowy street outside Remi's apartment building where he'd lucked into a parking spot. He started the vehicle and let it run to warm up a bit, the fan blowing on the windshield. In the wintery evening night, he sat there for a long time, his fast breaths blowing puffs of white into the cold night air.

He was drawn back to Emily. Against his will. Against his better judgment. He knew she wasn't his daughter, but he still felt responsible. Still felt a sense of duty. And Brianne…he didn't love her anymore, but there was still a link between them, a link because of Emily.

He knew in his head that it wasn't really a link. Emily wasn't his daughter. Brianne was nothing to him. But he'd held Emily, smiled down at her and started to fall in love with her. Knowing she wasn't his biological child didn't change that.

It should. He knew it should.

Fuck. He was messed up inside, his head full of crazy, mixed-up ideas that shouldn't even be there. In the rational part of his brain, he knew he should be walking away from this, from Brianne and Emily. Emily had a father and it wasn't him.

He thought about how exhausted Brianne had looked. How she'd sent her mother home because she was doing too much for the baby when Brianne wanted to look after her herself. A surge of warmth toward Brianne rose inside him. Who knew she'd feel that kind of maternal love for her child? Despite his denials to her, he was surprised. He'd been afraid she wouldn't be the greatest mother in the world. That she'd be more concerned about her career or her looks than about her child. But apparently she wasn't.

She sure hadn't been concerned about her looks when he'd been there earlier.

And that kind of made him feel…softer toward her. He wanted to hate her for lying to him. For leading him down this path to where he felt such a strong sense of duty and responsibility that he wanted to be a father with every cell of his being.

Fuck! He was nuts. He flexed his gloved fingers around the

steering wheel and put the SUV into drive, even though he wasn't sure where he was going.

It didn't seem weird that he wanted to be a father, even though he was young. Most of the guys on the team were married and had kids, and many of them were his age or younger. They'd all talked about why hockey players seemed to get married young, and he remembered one of the wives saying that it was because hockey players usually left home at a pretty young age. He'd been seventeen when he moved to another province to play junior hockey, and he'd been independent and on his own ever since. He'd had his share of fun as a single guy. Remi'd tried to tell him what they'd be missing by not being able to go out and party all the time, but the truth was, all that partying no longer appealed to him as it once had.

Okay, he knew this was ironic. He'd broken up with Brianne because he hadn't wanted to be tied down. Committed. Marriage had scared the hell out of him. And then he'd met Remi and all he'd wanted in the world was to be with her. Forever.

That hadn't meant kids. That hadn't even been in his mind when he'd realized he loved her and wanted to spend the rest of his life with her. But now... He dragged a gloved hand back over his hair.

And found himself stopped in front of Brianne's elegant condo just off Michigan Avenue.

CHAPTER SIX

The Wolves won the next night, and Jason got a goal on a breakaway that was sweet as Christmas candy. The atmosphere in the dressing room was festive as everyone got into holiday mode, many of the players and their families travelling for Christmas to be with family, and the victory added to the good cheer.

It was hard to feel down after the win and the goal and all the trash talking with the other guys, but as Jase left the arena later to head home, some of his heaviness returned. He hadn't talked to Remi all day after he'd walked out last night. They were supposed to fly to Winnipeg the next morning, Christmas Eve. He wanted to just go to her place to see her but he had to finish packing. So he went home, but once inside the house, he phoned her. "Hey," he said.

"Hi." She paused. "Where are you?"

"Home."

"Oh. Already?"

"Yeah. Had to finish packing. Were you at the game?"

"No." She paused. "I didn't feel like going tonight, so I watched on TV."

"Oh." Disappointment filtered through him. He always liked knowing she was there with the other wives and girlfriends, cheering him on. "I got a goal."

"Yeah. I saw it. You guys played great tonight."

"So…tomorrow. I'll need to pick you about eight o'clock."

Silence. "You still want me to go with you?" she finally said.

"Of course! What are you talking about?"

"You walked out the other night, and never called me yesterday. What am I supposed to think? Are we breaking up?"

"No." His voice went rough. "Christ, no, Remi. I love you."

"Maybe you should go home for Christmas alone. We'll figure this out when you're back."

"I'm not going without you. We've already booked our flights and my family's expecting us."

"Well, we certainly wouldn't want to disappoint them." Her voice acquired a faint edge.

Damn. "Remi. That's not the only reason. I don't want to leave things like this between us over Christmas. Come on, baby."

After a long silence she said, "Okay."

"I'll pick you up in the morning. I'll be there about eight. Okay?"

"I'll be ready."

And she was. When he walked in a few minutes after eight the next morning, she was standing beside her biggest suitcase wearing a blue turtleneck sweater, black wool pants and her spiky-heeled black boots, with her long winter coat already on.

They looked at each other and his heart gave a kick at seeing the wariness and sadness in her eyes. And then he opened his arms and she was in them. He wrapped his arms around her, her small body bulkier in the warm coat, and pressed her face to his chest.

"Jase."

"Remi. I'm sorry. I'm sorry if I've been pushing too hard. I love you."

"I know. I love you too."

She shifted in his arms and went onto her toes to kiss him. He bent and pulled her up on his body, his mouth covering hers in a long, blistering kiss. Her hands slid into his hair and he wished they weren't both wearing big coats. When they broke apart, their eyes met and Jase leaned his forehead against hers. "C'mon. Let's go."

The flight was short. They drank the coffee and ate the muffin they were served by a flight attendant who was doing her best to flirt with him even though Remi sat right there next to him.

"Ignore her," he whispered to her at one point. "I am."

"Ignore who?" she said.

They shared a smile. Things would be okay. They had to be okay. He fucking hated this strain between them. He wasn't giving up on convincing Remi to move in with him or to think about starting a family sooner rather than later. Which reminded him of his visit to Brianne the other night and seeing Emily again. "Hey," he said. "Emily's growing really fast."

Remi turned her small, heart-shaped face to look at him. "What?"

"Emily," he said again. "She already weighs nine pounds."

Remi blinked. "Did you see her?" Her forehead puckered.

"At Brianne's. I went there the other night."

She went very still and her turquoise eyes narrowed. "You went to Brianne's? After you left my place?"

Uh-oh. Jase had a feeling he was in trouble.

"Of course I'm nervous about meeting your family."

Logan grinned. "You've met my parents."

Nicole swatted his chest. They sat side by side in first class on the plane from Minneapolis to Winnipeg on Christmas Eve. "Oh, and I'm sure I made a great impression," she said. "Nearly passing out on them."

"You were that worried about me, huh? Aw."

"I thought you were dead."

A few weeks ago, he'd been driving hard toward the net in the game against the Chicago Wolves and somehow had crashed into the net. He'd been practically carried off the ice and Nicole had been terrified he was going to die with things all messed up between them. Before she'd admitted to him that she was in love with him.

His parents had been at the game because his brother Jason played for the Wolves, and they'd been as worried as she had, rushing down to the dressing room to check on him. So yeah, she'd met them, but it hadn't been under the best circumstances.

She'd liked them, though, his mom calm under pressure, his dad not saying much but equally as strong—strong and silent.

"I know a great cure for nerves," he murmured near her ear.

She gave a tiny shiver. "What?"

"Three words—mile high club."

Laughter bubbled up inside her. "As if."

"We could try it."

She shook her head, smiling. "Spending Christmas with your whole family is as intimidating as hell."

He snorted. "Riiiiiight, Miss Lambert. Who's your father again?"

She gave him a look. Yes, her father was a hockey legend and now an influential team owner in the NHL. Even so, that didn't give her a whole lot of confidence when it came to dealing with another hockey royalty family, the Hellers.

"We're not even a little intimidating," Logan continued. "We're fun and you'll fit right in." He leaned toward her and smooched her lips.

"Okay," she said. "I'm good. Good, good, good." She reached for her purse stowed under the seat in front of her and pulled out a lip gloss. She swiped some on her lips, dug around in her purse for something…hell, she couldn't remember what. She shoved the purse back under the seat. Oh yeah, gum. She needed gum for the landing. She hauled the purse out and pawed around in it again.

"Jesus," Logan muttered. "What are you doing?"

"I need gum. Want some gum? Gum's good when you're landing. Don't your ears hurt?"

"Nicole." He leaned toward her again. "Relax."

"I am. This was a short flight. We barely got up in the air and we started coming down."

His lips quirked. "Yup."

"So…Matt's already home." Matt was Logan's youngest brother.

"Yes."

"And Tag is already there of course." He lived in Winnipeg.

"And Kyla."

"Right. What's she like?"

"Mmm…very smart. Assertive. Ambitious. She's a lawyer."

"I knew that. Sounds like a ball breaker."

He choked on a laugh and smiled at her. "Yeah…no."

"And Jason and Remi are flying in today too, right?"

"Right. They should be there just before us."

"And what's Remi like?"

"Remi's very sweet. She's a teacher."

Great. A saintly teacher and a ball-breaker lawyer. She'd fit right in, sure.

Logan squeezed her hand, lifting it to nuzzle her knuckles. She could do this. She and Logan had only been together for just over a month, and meeting the whole family for Christmas kind of seemed like rushing things. But then, Logan had been pretty determined from the day they'd met that they were going to be together. And she had to admit…she liked it. She liked how much he wanted her. And she wanted him too.

"I've never been to Winnipeg."

"You'll love it."

She gave him a look, chin down. "Winterpeg?"

He laughed. "Oh come on. You're Canadian too. You can handle a little snow and cold. And Minneapolis is no different."

She grinned. "True."

"Mom's got a big dinner planned for the family tonight," he said. "Just family. An early dinner before we go to church tonight. "

"But you're not Catholic."

His lips twitched. "No. And you're a little lapsed. You'll survive the Lutheran Service. Christmas day will be just family again."

"Just family. Only nine of us."

"Hmm. Why are there only two kids in your good Catholic family?"

She smiled at him. God, she loved him. He was totally taking her mind off how nervous she was. "My mom's not Catholic. She's a model."

He burst out laughing. "Oh, I didn't know that was a religion of the world."

Their eyes met, his sparkling with amusement. He touched his fingers to her cheek.

"I mean, she totally believes in birth control," Nicole said.

"Ah. Me too."

"And me," she added fervently.

"Anyway, nine isn't bad. How many people were at Taylor and Fedor's for Thanksgiving?"

"That was different. This is important." She met his eyes again earnestly. "I want them to like me."

"They will like you, babe." He lifted the hand he held and kissed it. "Like I do."

The wheels of the plane bumped the ground and Nicole started. *"Câlisse.* We're here already. Okay." She took a deep breath. "Let's go do this."

Logan rented a vehicle at the airport and they made the short drive from there to his parent's home. She looked out the windows with interest at snow-bank-lined streets and buildings. Soon he turned off a major route into a residential neighborhood, the street lined with an arched canopy of bare black tree branches that created a quiet, cozy feel. Large houses were set well back from the street, the front yards an expanse of smooth white, many of the houses lavishly decorated with wreaths and garlands and bows.

He parked on the street in front of a big, two-story Colonial-style house, the driveway already full of vehicles. "That's it," he said with a nod.

Her body tightened and she took a breath as she opened the door. Logan grabbed their suitcases and easily carried both up to the front door. Two small Christmas trees in urns flanked the door on the wide veranda and a huge wreath adorned with red ribbons, pine cones and holly hung on the door. He opened it and stepped inside, lugging the suitcases and banging against the doorframe. "We're here!" he called out.

Nicole followed along behind him, trying not to bite her lips.

Laura Heller appeared in the wide hall with a big smile on her face. "Hello! You made it!" She gave her son a hug, her pleasure evident on her youthful face. "And Nicole! I'm so glad you're here!" Nicole moved in for a hug too, a warm, genuine hug, and she smiled.

"Thank you for having me, Mrs. Heller," she said.

"Call me Laura. And you are very welcome." Laura shot Logan an amused glance. "This time we'll get to meet you properly and get to know you better." She looked back to Logan. "How's the shoulder?"

"It's good. Perfect."

She lifted an eyebrow and Nicole rolled her eyes. "So he says," she said.

"Uh-huh." Laura nodded. "Well, come in and meet Jase and Remi." Nicole almost missed the flicker of something that crossed Laura's face when she said their names, her mouth tightening just a bit. "They just got here a little while ago. And Matt's here. Tag and Kyla will be over later. Let me take your coats."

She hung their jackets in a closet while they removed their boots, then led the way down the hall and into a big kitchen that overlooked a sunken family room. Big windows in the far wall flooded the room with wintery white sunshine reflected off the snowy yard behind the house. More wreaths hung against the mullioned panes, suspended by wide red ribbons, and in the corner a huge spruce tree twinkled with lights and decorations. The room smelled faintly of wood smoke from the fire burning in a stone fireplace and the scent of the spruce tree.

Nicole greeted Logan's dad Doug again, then turned to his brothers Matt and Jason, whom she easily recognized. All four boys had a similar look, Matt's face thinner and younger, although he had that same charming Heller grin. Matt and Jason gave her warm hugs.

"Good to meet you," Jason said, giving her an assessing up-and-down look that some might have thought flirtatious, but which she recognized as sizing up whether she was good enough for his brother.

"You too," she said.

"And this is Remi," Jason said, drawing forward a tiny blonde woman. Nicole felt like a giant beside Remi's delicate beauty, but man, for such a pretty woman her face wore a bitchy expression, the corners of her mouth tight and her eyes dull.

"Hi," Remi said coolly, extending a hand to shake. "It's great to meet you."

Her lack of enthusiasm made Nicole's insides tighten, but she smiled and shook the little blonde's hand. Then Remi turned to give Logan a hug and Nicole watched with narrowed eyes.

They made some small talk about their flights and the weather while Logan's mom moved into the kitchen and busied herself preparing something. Remi separated herself from the group as well and took a seat in a big leather armchair, quiet and unsmiling. Nicole cast her a wary glance, then smiled and answered Jason's questions about the flight. Logan and Jason then started talking about Jase's game the night before and his goal.

"I'm just getting some lunch ready," Laura said from the kitchen. "But, Logan, you can take your suitcases upstairs and show Nicole where you'll be staying."

Nicole caught Logan's eye. She hadn't given a thought to the sleeping arrangements. Were Logan's parents going to put them in separate bedrooms?

"Come on, Nic," he said easily, tipping his head and extending a hand. "I'll give you a tour of the house."

He led her back into the hallway. As soon as they were out of the room, she felt a lightening of tension. She took a deep breath. She'd been nervous enough about meeting the whole family, but she hadn't expected Remi to outright hate her and ignore her.

"The family room's an addition," Logan explained. "A two-story addition. The upstairs is a master suite for my parents. Living room...dining room...den...powder room..." He grabbed the suitcases he'd left in the foyer and nodded for Nicole to precede him up the stairs. She reached for the big wooden newel post and climbed the steps, beautiful polished oak lined with a patterned runner in shades of green and taupe.

"The house is beautiful," she said, admiring all the framed photographs on the moss green wall, arranged in seemingly random fashion. At the bend in the stairs, a window with big oak casing and a generous sill let in more of the bright sunshine, and at the top of the stairs she faced a wide hall.

"Five bedrooms," he said. "One for each of us when they added the master suite. This is the big bathroom," he said. "We'll have it mostly to ourselves, but we'll have to share with Matt. He's staying in his room there." He nodded at a closed door. "That room's Tag's, but I understand he pretty much lives with Kyla now. Jase and Remi are staying in Jase's old room, which has an attached bathroom. And this is my old room." He led the way into a spacious bedroom that held a king-size bed, an antique oak dresser, a mismatched maple armoire and an upholstered armchair big enough for two. The walls were painted a burgundy red color that made Nicole blink, but it was really gorgeous with the golden oak window frames and floor.

"Nice," she said. "Did you pick this color?"

"Nah. Mom redecorated it a few years ago. I used to spend summers here, but the last few years those visits have gotten shorter, and I stayed in California most of the time."

She pursed her lips and sat on the burgundy-and-navy patterned duvet on the bed. "What will you do this year?"

He smiled at her. "Stay in Minneapolis, I guess."

Logan had been traded only a couple of months ago in a surprise deal that had moved him from California to Minnesota. Even though he'd made the best of it, she knew he still missed his beach home.

"Minneapolis is fun in the summer."

"It will be if you're there."

"Sweet talker."

He grinned and gave her a little push, sending her to her back on the bed. He bent over her, supporting his weight on his arms. "You betcha. Wanna have a quickie?"

"All you think about is sex," she complained, flattening her palms on his chest. "Okay."

He laughed.

"What? You were kidding?" She shoved at his chest with mock anger. "Sure, get me all excited and then let me down."

"Just wait." He straightened, grabbed her hands and pulled her to her feet and up against him. "I packed some toys. And check out that headboard."

A smile tugging her lips, she turned to look. "Mmm. I see." The oak headboard fit right into the room with square posts and solid spindles. "It'll be perfect for tying you up later."

"Ha." His hands went to her ass and pulled her closer. "Not gonna happen, babe. It'll be *you* at *my* mercy."

Her tummy did a little lust flip and she dragged her tongue over her bottom lip.

Logan groaned and gave her a smack on one butt cheek. He hit the sweet spot where it was more pleasure than pain, and heat flared inside her. "C'mon. Let's get back to the family."

Now it was her turn to groan. "Your brother's girlfriend hates me," she said. "I don't want to go back down there." Her stomach returned to its knotted state.

"What?" Logan's mouth fell open. "She doesn't hate you."

"Yes, she does. She was a total bitch to me down there."

He stared at her. Then he rubbed his forehead. "She was kind of quiet. But she's not a bitch. And she can't hate you, she just met you."

Nicole pursed her lips. "Fine. If you say so." She forced a smile and took Logan's arm. "Let's go."

CHAPTER SEVEN

Kyla and Tag arrived at his parents' home in the late afternoon of Christmas Eve, ready to have dinner with his whole family and then go to church. Tag parked in the driveway of her parents' home across the street from his parents' place. Her parents were away in Vancouver having Christmas with her brother and his family.

"Looks like there's a party going on," Tag said with a grin, surveying the vehicles lining the narrow residential street.

"Well, I guess there is."

Tag's good mood was a little hard to handle when she was so stressed. She knew he was happy to be seeing all his brothers again. They'd all been together in the summer and it had been so much fun. The Hellers were like her own family, since she'd grown up across the street from them, and their families had lake cottages side by side where they'd spent most of their summers.

When she thought about it, it was a little amazing that the boys she'd followed around the neighborhood, the boys who'd taught her to skate and play baseball and how to water ski at the lake, were now famous, wealthy professional athletes. She'd known growing up that they were all talented hockey players, everyone had known that, but making it into the NHL wasn't easy and all four of them had done it. Well, Matt hadn't yet played his first NHL game, but he'd been drafted and it wouldn't be long before he was ready to make that move.

She pressed a hand to her abdomen as they walked up the sidewalk.

Inside, the house was loud and testosterone-laden with all the big hunky hockey players. She greeted Matt with a fond hug, happy to see him home from college in North Dakota, then Jase and Remi.

"So nice to see you," Kyla whispered to Remi as they embraced. "I heard the news…you must be so relieved."

Remi met her eyes and gave a brief nod. "I am," she admitted. "But…" She bit her lip and cast a sideways glance at Jase.

Kyla tipped her head in question, but there was no opportunity for a private chat just then.

Then Logan was greeting her. They hugged and he stepped back to introduce her to Nicole. "This is Kyla MacIntosh," he said. "Kyla, Nicole."

"Nice to meet you," Kyla said, trying for enthusiasm despite her distracted mood. She really was happy to see Remi and to meet Nicole. She'd been the only girl with all the guys all those years. It would be nice to have more female company. "Welcome to Winnipeg."

"Thanks," Nicole said quietly with a small smile.

Kyla drifted to the kitchen to help Tag's mom, watching affectionately as Tag reconnected with his brothers and his dad. They were all so pumped to see each other, it was really cute.

"How's work?" Laura asked.

Kyla turned her attention to Laura as she pulled a tray of appetizers out of the stove. "Are those sausage rolls? Tag loves those."

"I know." Laura smiled.

"Work is good," Kyla said, her shoulders tightening thinking about it. "It's nice to have a few days off."

"You look a little tense. Some time off will be good for you."

Laura was too damn perceptive. Kyla pasted on a smile and grabbed a serving platter.

Remi tried to focus on all the family stuff going on around her, but her body felt stiff, her mind blurry. After Jase had told her just as they were landing that he'd gone to visit Brianne and Emily again, they'd barely had time to talk. His dad had been waiting for them in the airport to drive them home and they were soon surrounded by the Hellers.

Why had he done that?

She kept asking herself the question over and over. She looked at him talking to his brothers and laughing. What was going on with him? This whole baby thing was crazy. And her thoughts started getting crazy too, crazy and fearful and anxious.

Then Kyla and Tag arrived. There were more hugs and greetings and catching up. Remi liked Kyla. She was gorgeous and smart, a lawyer who looked like Kate Beckinsale, and they'd gotten to be friends when they'd met last summer.

So she was happy to see Kyla again and gave her a tight hug. Maybe there'd be a chance to talk to Kyla about what was happening with Jase. Although she was Tag's girlfriend, she'd known Jase since they were kids, and she might have some insight into why he was acting so weird.

What if he wanted a baby so bad he was willing to go back to Brianne to get that? Even if the baby wasn't his.

No, that was just insane. She couldn't believe she'd actually had that thought. But her mind whirled and she couldn't ignore the ache in her heart from hearing he'd gone to see Brianne.

It was bad enough he'd had to see Brianne when they thought

the baby was his. But now they knew he wasn't Emily's father, *why?* There was no reason whatsoever that he had to go visit them!

When he'd walked into her apartment that morning, she'd been filled with so much love for him, and she been so relieved when he'd opened his arms to her. On the plane, she'd been hopeful that things would be okay and had almost been ready to tell him her news, when he'd dropped that bomb on her.

Good thing she hadn't told him. She'd been thinking a lot about it, trying to decide if she should tell him before Christmas or surprise him on Christmas morning. Things were a big mess, but now she was glad she hadn't said anything.

Her stomach lurched again. Mrs. Heller was setting out more food, which the guys devoured as quickly as it appeared, but she could barely eat two bites.

"Nice goal last night," Tag said to Jase. "Apparently Farrell was thinking about where he was going for drinks after the game." He referred to the Rockies' goalie.

"Shut up. I completely had him. He was looking for the poke check and I went top shelf. It was beautiful."

"You were lucky," Tag said with a grin, then gave his brother a light punch in the shoulder.

"That was not luck. That was pure skill. How many games has it been since you scored a goal?" Jase asked his older brother.

Tag's smile disappeared. Remi knew Tag hadn't had a goal in quite a few games and the media was all over it. But she also knew these brothers loved each other a lot, despite knowing what buttons to push.

More hockey talk ensued, talk about the phenomenal fan support the Jets were getting in their first season back in Winnipeg and a lot of talk about Logan's trade to Minneapolis, his injury and his being made captain.

Remi tried to pay attention, keeping a smile fixed firmly in place and nodding occasionally, but her mind kept wandering and the hard knot of anger and hurt in her stomach distracted her. And Jase was so wrapped up in seeing his brothers again that he'd barely even looked at her.

She looked down at the glass of eggnog in her hand and blinked.

She did not want to be there.

She relaxed briefly during the Christmas Eve church service, enjoying singing familiar carols as the strong beautiful voices of the choir soared above the congregation's to the dark rafters of the candlelit church. But now as they all walked home from church in the dark, walking two by two along the snow-covered sidewalk, boots crunching the snow in rhythm and their breath forming puffs of white in the air, the tension returned. Despite the beauty all around them in the frosty dark, the tension that swirled and thickened made her insides hurt. She breathed cold air into her lungs.

Jason reached for her gloved hand and she resisted the urge to pull it away. They hadn't had a chance to be alone all day and she was still tied up in knots over the fact that he'd gone to see Brianne and her baby. On top of that, Logan's new girlfriend Nicole appeared to hate her. She was tall, model-gorgeous and athletic. Remi had no idea why she seemed to have taken an instant dislike to her. And even worse, there seemed to be something going on between Tag and Kyla. It wasn't big and tremendously obvious, but Remi caught them sharing edgy looks, and Kyla's eyes had gone distant and her mouth thin a few times.

Merry Christmas to all.

Once back at the Heller house, a flurry of activity ensued as everyone removed coats and jackets and boots and gloves, then congregated again in the great room. Jase's mom set out plates of appetizers and cookies while his dad served drinks. Kyla helped as if she'd grown up in the house, which she kind of had, and

Remi and Nicole sat on chairs next to each other. Remi looked at Nicole, all long, sexy legs in a short skirt and sweater, holding a drink.

"So. Um. I hear you played hockey," she said.

Nicole gave her a cool smile. "I did. Back in university and high school."

"That's really awesome. Laura played hockey too."

"That's what Logan told me. Are you going to come play with us tomorrow at the community center?"

"God no!"

Nicole blinked and drew back.

"I mean, I'll come and skate around a bit, but I can't play hockey. I'll be lucky if I can stay upright." That wasn't completely true. She'd taken skating lessons as a girl, so she could skate, but she knew she was in no league with Nicole or Mrs. Heller.

"I'm sure it won't be anything serious," Nicole said with a shrug. "Hey, Kyla. You coming to the community center tomorrow?"

"Sure." Kyla set a plate of cookies on the coffee table.

"We could play guys against the girls," Nicole suggested.

Oh god. Remi would totally let down the girls in any team effort. She wasn't athletic like Nicole, and she knew how competitive Kyla was. If Nicole played hockey, she was probably aggressive and competitive too.

Kyla laughed. "Sure. We can beat a bunch of NHL players. No problem."

Remi let out a breath. Obviously she was taking this way too seriously.

"We can't play guys against the girls," Matt said, sitting on the couch with a beer in one hand and a cookie in the other. "We outnumber you."

"That's because you don't have a girlfriend," Jase pointed out. He made an 'L' shape with his fingers in front of his forehead.

Matt grinned.

"It's true," Laura said, smiling. "You need a girlfriend, Matt, so we have even teams."

"You're not playing hockey tomorrow," Tag said to Kyla.

She went very still as her hand reached for a cookie. She turned and gave him a look that had Remi blinking. "Yes, I am."

"No, you're not." Tag's voice went low and hard.

Kyla shot a glance around the room and shifted in her chair. "Tag…"

"Kyla…"

There was that tension Remi'd noticed earlier between the two of them. Everyone in the room was staring at them, the air now thick.

"What the hell, Tag," Jase said. "She can play if she wants."

"No. She can't." Tag's jaw set and his lips compressed.

Everyone started talking at once, the women trying to defend Kyla's right to play hockey if she wanted, the guys calling out Tag for being an asshole. Finally Tag stood, clutching his drink. His eyes flashed.

"Would you all just shut the hell up," he roared.

The room fell silent. Mouths dropped open and everyone stared at him.

"She's not playing hockey tomorrow because she's pregnant!" Tag shouted.

Kyla slumped back into her chair and covered her face. "Oh my god. Tag."

"What? It's true."

Remi suddenly felt as if she was watching from a distance. Kyla was pregnant?

And then she couldn't help but look at Jase. His face had gone slack, eyebrows slanted down, staring at Kyla. Remi pressed a hand to her stomach just as Jase turned to look at her and met her eyes. And the pain in his eyes made her insides constrict hard and her chest hurt.

"Tag. How could you?" Kyla sat up and Remi turned her gaze

back to her. Kyla had gone as white as the snow outside and her mouth had tightened as she glared at Tag. "How could you tell everyone like that? We haven't even…" Her lips pressed together and she squeezed her eyes closed briefly. Then she stood and rushed from the room.

More silence followed her hasty exist. The tension in the room had passed uncomfortable and climbed all the way up to excruciating. Remi looked at the faces in the room—Nicole and Logan exchanging surprised glances, Mr. and Mrs. Heller looking more concerned. Tag's face darkened and he gulped some of his drink. And Jase… Jase looked like someone had just ripped out his heart.

Remi closed her eyes as despair washed through her. Goddammit! As if he wasn't hurt enough by not being a father, now his brother was going to have a baby. How was he going to handle that? And was that going to mean even more pressure on her to do the same?

Kyla didn't know where she was running to, but she couldn't stay in the room. Fury at Tag welled up inside her, as well as humiliation. She ended up in the main floor powder room, sitting on the closed toilet, her face in her hands.

Damn him! Godfreakingdamn him. Why had he said that to everyone?

Frustration mingled with the anger, and she dug her fingertips into her skull. Then she took a deep breath and reached for some bathroom tissue to wipe the tears that dampened her eyes. She rubbed her mouth and looked up at the ceiling. Shit.

A soft knock sounded on the door.

She swallowed. "Who is it?"

"Me. Tag."

Her bottom lip quivered. "Come in."

The door knob turned and Tag entered the room.

He filled the small space with his big body. He closed the door behind him and leaned on it. For a moment, he said nothing and she watched his eyes flicker and his mouth move. "Kyla," he said. "Don't do this."

"Don't do what? You shouldn't have told them!"

He closed his eyes. "I'm sorry. It slipped out. But they have to know."

"They don't have to know! What if...what if..." Her throat closed up.

He dropped to his knees in front of her and grabbed her hands. "Kyla. Were you serious this morning? When you said you weren't sure if you wanted to have this baby?"

CHAPTER EIGHT

"I don't know." Kyla pleaded with her eyes for understanding, turning her hands to grip his too. "I don't know, Tag."

"Why?" His fingers squeezed tighter.

"I just don't know if this is the right time to have a baby. I just made partner. After what I had to go through to get this, what are they going to think if I announce I'm pregnant and want to go on maternity leave?"

"Who the fuck cares what they think?"

She lowered her chin, holding his gaze. "I care. It's my career."

"Fuck," he muttered. "You should've taken that job with the Jets."

She sighed. "Maybe. I don't know. I thought I was doing the right thing. I didn't want to give up on everything I'd worked so hard for at Ingram Howell Grant. And I had a feeling working for a hockey team was going to be another boys' club. But I've been doing better…haven't I? About balancing work and home."

"Yeah. You have. Kyla, don't you want kids? Some day? I know we haven't talked about it, but damn…"

"Seriously? Do we really have to have this conversation in a bathroom? With your whole family out there wondering what the hell is going on?"

He groaned and rose to his feet. He tugged her up and into his arms, crushing her in a tight hug. "Yeah. I'm sorry. Shit."

"Could we go home and talk?"

"Yeah." He rubbed his face on her hair then nudged her head until he found her mouth with his. His warm kiss eased the tension in her body. "Let's go home, Mac."

His old nickname for her made her heart soften.

God. This was not how she'd planned her life. But they had to deal with it.

"I so don't want to face your family right now." She hesitated. "After what just happened with Jase…your mom's going to be freaking out about being a grandma again."

Tag's mouth compressed. "She might. Shit. Look, go get your coat. Where's your purse?"

"It's with my coat in the front closet."

"Okay, good. I'll go excuse us. We'll see them tomorrow."

Her throat ached. "Thank you."

He kissed her again and opened the bathroom door. Kyla padded toward the front of the house while Tag disappeared into the back. She heard the voices as she put her coat on and tugged on her high-heeled boots. Tag reappeared as she wound a big scarf around her neck.

"Okay?" she asked.

"Yup." He donned his black car coat and they let themselves out into the frosty night.

The overcast sky was luminous, reflecting back the lights of the city and the snow. Fat flakes had begun to fall, drifting slowly through the air. The snow on the ground sparkled in the light of the streetlamp. Kyla turned her face up and snowflakes landed on her cheeks with a cool, gentle touch. "It's Christmas Eve snow," she murmured. "Perfect Christmas Eve snow."

Tag paused, standing in the middle of the narrow residential street. Lights twinkled on every house, and the neighborhood was quiet under the white blanket of snow. "You're beautiful," he said. "I love you, Kyla."

Her chest squeezed and she leaned against him. "I love you too."

"Let's go home."

Home was her place. Tag had pretty much moved into her Exchange District condo. He'd been looking for a house in Winnipeg since the team moved back, but somehow that had fallen by the wayside and he'd spent more and more time at her place, more and more of his belongings making their way there. And she loved it.

There was a lot to talk about. They'd only been together six months. They hadn't talked about marriage or kids or anything like that. Those were big things. Important things. Her shoulders tightened as they climbed into the cold car. Tag let it warm up for a minute before backing out of her parents' driveway onto the street.

As they headed downtown, few cars travelled the streets. The snowfall increased, but not enough to making driving difficult. Tag parked in the underground parking lot and they took the elevator up to her condo in the old converted warehouse.

"I need a drink," Tag said once they were in and their jackets and boots off. "Want something? Wine?"

She opened her mouth to say yes, please, and then remembered. "No," she said. "I can't drink."

He paused with his hand on the fridge door. "Oh yeah."

She sighed. "I want to change."

She turned on the gas fireplace in the living room and walked into the bedroom to take off the black dress she'd worn to church. She stripped off black tights and then what the hell, her bra too, and slipped into pajamas, a pair of red and green flannel pants and a snug, red, long-sleeved T-shirt with the word 'naughty' across the front.

Tag appeared just as she smoothed the shirt down over her stomach, and her hand lingered there. Was there really a life growing in there? It was almost incomprehensible.

Tag approached her and laid his hand on top of hers. He looked into her eyes. "I can hardly believe it."

"I know," she whispered. "I was just thinking that. God, Tag. It scares the crap out of me."

"Hey, me too." His lips quirked. "Go sit down. I made you a hot chocolate."

Her heart squeezed. "Aw. Thank you."

She found the steaming mug on the coffee table. Tag had turned on a side lamp and the glow of the gas fireplace created a cozy feel. Through the big arched window in the old brick wall she could see the snow still falling.

Tag returned, also in a pair of plaid flannel pants and a white V-necked shirt that showed off his killer body—his wide shoulders, muscled chest and flat abs. Her heart beat a little faster. He was so freakin' gorgeous.

He sat beside her and picked up another mug.

"I thought you were having beer."

He shrugged. "If you can't drink for nine months, I won't either."

Her bottom lip quivered. Love for him swelled up inside her. She sipped her chocolate, afraid to point out that she hadn't decided for sure if she was going to be pregnant for nine months. But then a cold feeling swept through her and she closed her eyes.

"Okay," he said. "Let's talk. First of all…will you marry me?"

Nicole watched Kyla rush out of the room. Everyone sat there, not sure where to look. Or what to say apparently, as thick silence filled the great room.

"Pregnant?" Mrs. Heller said. "Oh dear."

"Here we go again, "Jase muttered. "For fuck's sake."

"Jason." His mother gave him a frown.

Nicole's already stretched-taut nerves began to fray. She'd been nervous about meeting Logan's family when they'd only been together such a short time. She wanted them to like her, and it seemed like they didn't, or at least Kyla and Remi didn't. Add this little family drama to the mix and it was a bit much. She licked her bottom lip and stole a glance at Logan.

He sat there with a slack jaw and blinking eyes too. Their eyes met. She moved her head and looked toward the door, trying to ask him if she should leave, but he just frowned.

Nicole looked at Remi and the stricken expression on her face gave her pause. She watched Remi and Jase exchange fulminating glances. Yikes.

Then Mrs. Heller turned into her husband's arms and buried her face in his neck.

"I-I think I'll go up to bed," Nicole said, rising to her feet. She carried her wineglass into the kitchen and poured what was left into the sink, then set the glass in the dishwasher. She made a hasty exit and climbed the stairs into the sanctuary of Logan's old room.

She sat on the bed. So Kyla was pregnant. But why had she run out like that? Didn't she want people to know? Nicole supposed it was common for people to wait until after the first trimester to make their announcement, but who knew how far along Kyla was. She didn't look pregnant, that was for sure.

The bedroom door opened and Logan walked in. He quietly closed the door behind him.

"Hey," he said, frowning. "What's wrong?"

"I shouldn't have come here."

He sat beside her on the bed and reached for her hands. "No! Why do you say that?"

"I just feel like I'm in the way. There's all kinds of family drama going on. The tension is killing me. I want your family to like me, and Kyla and Remi seem to hate my guts and now everyone's all freaked out about Kyla being pregnant."

Logan shook his head. "They don't hate your guts! Why would you say that?"

She shrugged and looked down at their joined hands. "Just a feeling I get. Remi's snooty. Kyla's bitchy."

"She's pregnant."

"That's no excuse."

Logan was silent and his fingers rubbed over hers.

"Your parents are really nice, but they're distracted about the news about Jase. Everything's just a big mess. I wish I wasn't here."

"Oh, Nic, don't say that. I want you here. I need you here."

He wrapped his arms around her and she cuddled into him. "Thank you," she whispered. "But I don't know how I'm going to get through the next few days with things like this. Christmas is supposed to be fun and happy."

He rubbed her back. "Yeah. It is. But I'm happy. We're happy. Right?"

She nodded against him. "Sort of."

"I'm sorry, hon. You're right. This isn't the best trip for you. It's weird. My family's usually pretty low key. We're all easygoing guys."

"It's all the women," she joked. "We're messing things up for you."

"Huh." He fell silent.

She lifted her head. "I was joking."

"Well. It's sort of true."

She frowned.

"I mean, not that you're messing things up," he continued hastily. "It just adds a whole other layer to things. We've always been a guy family, other than my mom. She's pretty good at dealing with guy shit. She was so happy when Tag and Kyla got together because she'd finally have a daughter. She was thrilled when she thought she was going to be a grandma. But having more people in the family does make things more complicated."

"So I was right. I shouldn't have come." She tried to pull away.

He held on tighter. "That's not what I meant," he said evenly. "Calm down, Nic."

"Calm down?"

"Sorry, sorry. I know that's the wrong thing to say."

He wasn't even letting her start a good fight. God, she loved this man.

"You know what you need?"

"Um…what?"

He grabbed her legs and lifted them up across his lap, then reached for her hips and smoothly flipped her onto her stomach. His hand landed on her ass in a gently stinging swat.

"Hey!"

"You need a spanking," he said evenly, laying another smack on her other cheek.

Heat bloomed and spread over her ass. Logan shoved up the short, stretchy black skirt she wore and yanked her black tights down to her knees, leaving her bare to him save for her thong panties.

His palm molded to her buttock in a warm massage, then lifted to deliver another sharp pat, warming her bare skin. His hand found the perfect spot, the spot where pain met pleasure and made her pussy ache as he continued to spank her. A moan climbed up her throat and she fisted the bedspread, eyes squeezed closed.

"Is this what you need?" he growled, pausing to rub her hot skin.

"Yes," she whispered. Her hips lifted, silently begging for more and he obliged her. The burn intensified, a warm glow spread through her body and she let herself go, absorbing it, letting herself float away, letting her mind go dark and quiet.

His fingers pushed aside her panties and delved into her pussy. "Fuck yeah," he groaned. "You're wet."

She murmured her agreement, knowing she was wet by the intense ache there. Then he returned to spanking her, cupping his palm just right, hitting just the right spots to make her soar, pain and pleasure mingling in an edgy, euphoric luminance. The room faded away and all she was aware of was his hard thighs beneath her, his hand on her ass, and a delicious, hazy pleasure. The heat on her buttocks turned to a sweet throb that mingled with the throb behind her clit, and her hips lifted again, needily.

He rested his hands on her buttocks, holding them there. She felt herself pulsing, became aware of her breathing, her heartbeat as she drifted back down. Then Logan moved out from under her, stretching her out on the bed still face down. She felt him come down beside her and then he laid his lips on her heated flesh in a long, soft kiss. She sighed.

He rubbed his stubbled cheek over sensitized skin and a shiver worked over her body. Then he kissed her ass cheeks, letting his tongue stroke over her, down to the crease where buttock met thigh. Tingles floated through her veins and up her spine as he cupped her with big hands and kissed and licked. He pulled her panties off, down over her legs, along with the tights that were still around her ankles.

Then he guided her arms up over her head and wrapped her fingers around the wooden spindles of the headboard. "Hold on," he directed her, his voice low and rough. Her face buried against her upper arm, she floated along, barely aware of the rustling noises and movement, and then Logan's hands parted her thighs as he climbed between them. His fingers slid up and down through her slick folds, his other hand molding to the small of her back, pressing her down.

She loved it, loved the relief of surrendering to him, loved how he could strip everything away, leaving simplicity and clarity and freedom.

He slid a finger inside her and she tightened on him. Then his fingertips rubbed over her again, settling over her clit. She jerked and her fingers constricted on the wooden headboard. He rubbed there, and sensation gathered, her womb tightening. But he withdrew his hand and she whimpered.

"Not yet, baby. I'm gonna fuck you." And then she felt the big blunt head of his cock at her entrance, sliding up and down through her lips there then pushing into her. His knees pushed her legs farther apart and his hands gripped her hips, lifting her onto him as he slid in with exquisite fullness. "Ah yeah. So hot and wet. Tight on my dick. And your ass is such a pretty pink right now." He rubbed one cheek again. "Hold on, 'cause I wanna fuck you hard."

His voice grew hoarser with those last words and he kept his promise, driving into her with heavy penetration. So deep. Unbearable pleasure swelled inside her. She wanted to touch her clit, but he'd ordered her to hold on, and she curled her fingers tighter as he pounded into her from behind. She pushed back with her hips, wanting more, wanting it harder, the buzzing behind her clit straining for more. Then he slipped a hand around her, beneath her, found her clit and gently rubbed.

The thick slide of him in and out and the touch of his fingers on her clit combined to send her rocketing. She pressed her mouth to her arm to keep from crying out too loudly, even in her transported state aware that there were others in the house. Even so, strangled, muffled noises emerged from her lips as she burst into flames, blood throbbing through her body, nerve endings burning, her pussy contracting hard around his heavy shaft.

"Fuck yeah!" His fingers dug into her hips as he pressed himself hard against her, coming inside her in hot, liquid pulses. He fell forward over her, pressing himself to her back and opened his teeth gently on her shoulder, grunting with his release.

Long moments later, they separated and he rolled to his back.

Nicole released her grip on the spindle and flexed her fingers. Logan reached for the hand nearest to him, rubbed it, brought it to his lips to kiss her fingers. She shifted, barely able to move her lethargic body, to cuddle against him, and his other arm slid around her shoulders. Still holding her hand in his, they lay like that.

"You seem more relaxed now," he commented lazily.

She smiled against his chest. "Yep. I'm so relaxed I may never leave this bed. Just bring my presents up here tomorrow morning, okay?"

His fingers tangled in her hair and tugged her head back so he could kiss her. "No can do. Because I might not be able to get out of bed either."

CHAPTER NINE

Jase looked at Remi. Kyla'd gone running out of there, then Nicole. And Remi looked as if she was ready to throw up. Christ. That was kinda how he felt too.

Kyla was pregnant.

The news had hit him like a punch in the gut, knocking the wind out of him. He struggled to breathe normally, his hands curling into fists. *Fuck!*

That was just too cruel when he was trying to convince Remi to have a baby. And she didn't want to. Not that he didn't want Tag and Kyla to have a baby. He was happy for them. He was. It was just hard to be happy for someone else, when they had what you wanted so badly…

Christ, he was a selfish prick. He swallowed.

"I think I'll go upstairs too," Remi said quietly. "This seems like family stuff."

She disappeared. Tag excused himself to go after Kyla, and Logan followed Nicole upstairs. Jase sat there with Matt and his parents.

"What's everyone all upset about?" Matt asked, leaning back

in the couch, a crease between his eyebrows. He tipped his beer to his lips and drank.

"Oh man." Jase groaned. "You are so clueless."

Matt's eyebrows rose. "Yeah, thank god." He shook his head.

Jase looked over at his parents standing there with their arms around each other. He still felt as if he'd let his mom down in some weird way, disappointing her that she wasn't going to be a grandmother, even though it was in no way his fault. In hindsight, maybe he should have handled things differently. But now Tag, big brother, always the hero who could do no wrong, was the one who'd give her what she wanted.

He needed to talk to Remi about this. She was the one who could smack him around and make him see straight. She was the one who could keep him focused and on track. So he said good night too, and headed upstairs.

His old bedroom was empty, but he heard water running in the attached bathroom through the closed door. He unbuttoned his shirt as he moved across the room, tossed it over the chair in the corner then stripped off the rest of his clothes. The door opened and Remi emerged in her bra and panties. But when his gaze landed on her face, his chest tightened. She'd washed off her makeup but her eyes were pink and puffy, her nose a little red. Fuckit, she'd been crying.

"C'mere," he said holding a hand out to her.

She pressed her lips together and shook her head, walking around him to get to her suitcase. She pulled out a pair of flannel pajamas that made him roll his eyes. Christ, he hated when she wore those. He wanted her naked in his bed.

She kept her back to him as she changed, her shoulders tense and spine straight. Then she climbed into the big bed and huddled under the covers.

"What's wrong, Rem?"

Her heavy sigh pissed him off. There they went again.

"Fine. Give me the silent treatment. I'm not in the best mood right now either." He took his turn in the bathroom. When he returned to the bedroom, he flicked off the lamp and climbed between cool sheets. Once he'd settled into place, he became aware of Remi's body shaking. Oh for god's sake. Was she crying?

He rolled to his side and laid a hand on her back. "Remi. Come on. Talk to me."

"I don't think I can talk right now," she mumbled thickly. "It's all too much."

"We gotta talk. Are you upset about Kyla being pregnant?"

She jerked away and flipped to her back. "No! I'm happy for them!"

"Then what's the problem?"

"Oh my god! I can't believe you."

"Uh…"

"You went to see Brianne!" she cried softly. In the darkness he could just make out her big shadowy eyes and the sheen of tears. "How could you do that?"

"I didn't go see Brianne," he said slowly. "I went to see Emily."

She made a strangled sound. "*Why?* Why would you do that?"

"Because…I wanted to see her."

"She's not your daughter!"

He flinched. "I know that. Believe me, I know it."

"I don't understand you! Do you know how much that hurt me, hearing you'd gone there?"

He withdrew his hand. "I didn't mean to hurt you," he said stiffly. "I just wanted to see her. Brianne was having a hard time all alone, and it's not easy being a new mom, and I wanted to make sure Emily was okay."

"It sounds like it *was* about seeing Brianne," she said shortly.

"Fuck, Remi. I can't believe we're still having this conversation. I've tried to tell you how I feel. This isn't easy for me."

"Clearly."

"And now Kyla and Tag are having a baby," he said. "I mean,

I'm happy for them. But it just makes me want a family of my own even more."

"I knew it!" She flopped down onto her back. "I knew this was going to happen the minute we heard she was pregnant."

"What?"

"You're going to use that to pressure me even more to have a baby."

He struggled to find words. "I'm not. I won't. I..." He felt like his brain was cramping up and his chest ached. "Fuckit. I give up, Remi. I can't say or do anything right. I just..." All he wanted was to marry her and have a family with her. What was so wrong with that? Wasn't that what most women wanted? Didn't she love him enough to give him that? Christ! This was fucking hopeless.

He threw back the covers and climbed out of bed. Naked. So what. "I'll go sleep somewhere else," he muttered, and strode out of the room. Luckily Tag had gone with Kyla and his room sat empty. Also luckily, the bed was made up, so he climbed in. After some restless thrashing around and adjusting the covers and pillows, he lay there and stared into the darkness. It took a long time to fall asleep.

∼

"Marry you?" Kyla stared at Tag.

He nodded, holding her gaze. "Yeah."

Whoa. Married. Whoa.

He reached into the pocket of his flannel pants and then held out his hand palm up. The low light sparkled off diamonds and gold.

Her breath caught and she stared at it. "Oh my god."

"I went to get it today. After you told me about the pregnancy test. I wasn't sure exactly when I was going to ask you, but..." He paused to take a quick breath, blinking a few times. Kyla's heart turned over in her chest. "But I guess now's the time."

He reached for her left hand. "So? Will you?"

"Jesus, Tag." Her heart nearly exploded as it burst into a rapid rhythm. "Wait."

He paused, eyes shadowed. His fingers trembled ever so slightly holding her hand and the small gold ring. She drew in a shaky breath.

"Are you asking me to marry you because I'm pregnant?"

He took a moment to think. She waited. "I'm asking you to marry me *now* because you're pregnant," he finally said. "But I want to marry you no matter what."

A smile trembled on her lips. "Good answer."

One corner of his mouth lifted. "Thanks."

"Do you think we should talk about babies and having a family and what we each want, before we decide to get married? Those are big things."

His mouth firmed. "We can talk about those things, but it won't change the fact that I want to marry you. I love you."

Heat radiated through her chest. "I love you too. And I want to marry you."

"Thank Christ. Here, please put this on. You're scaring the shit out of me."

She smiled again and let him slide the ring onto her left ring finger. "It's a little loose."

"We'll get it sized. It was Christmas Eve and it was nuts at the jewelry store. Do you like it?" His eyebrows rose anxiously.

She held her hand out to study it. The center round diamond sparkled furiously, flanked by two slightly smaller diamonds, all three of them quite astonishingly large. The yellow gold setting was shiny and simple. "I love it," she whispered. "It's so beautiful."

He let out a breath. She leaned over and kissed him, slow and sweet.

"We've only been together six months," she said.

"We've known each other our whole lives."

"True."

"I know what I want, Kyla."

"You always do." She kissed him again. "So. About kids."

"Don't you want kids?"

"I do. I really do." She laid her hand on his cheek. "This has just thrown me for a loop. We didn't plan this."

"How'd this happen? You're on the Pill."

"Yeah. I…ah…might have forgotten to take my pill, back when the Holland case was going to trial and I was going crazy."

"Once?"

"Maybe twice."Her stomach tightened. "I'm sorry, Tag."

"Christ! Don't apologize! Stuff happens."

She nodded. But…pregnant. Her. A baby. Cripes. "Do you understand why I feel like this isn't the right time?"

"Yeah." He sighed and stroked a hand over her hair. "I do. I get it. But…I don't know if I can handle the alternative."

She drew in a long shaky breath. "I don't know if I can either," she admitted.

"Oh." This time he let out a really long gusty breath. "Oh, Kyla."

And then she started to cry. She shifted against him and slid her arms around his neck, and his big arms encircled her. Warm. Strong. Safe. "It's your baby," she sobbed into his chest. "I love you and I love your baby. I didn't want this now! But I love this baby."

He made a noise in his throat, and held her tighter.

"I'm scared, Tag."

"Me too, babe." His voice came out in a low rasp. "But we can do this. Together. Right?"

"Right." Her throat ached a little and she kissed his neck. "I love you so much. I'm sorry I've been a bitch about this."

"Not a bitch. It's a big deal."

"I like to plan things. I don't like stuff that I can't control."

He snorted. "Duh."

She smiled against his skin. "I do wish you hadn't told your family yet."

"I'm sorry. I screwed up."

"And…" She lifted her head to give him a narrow-eyed look. "Just because I'm pregnant doesn't mean I can't go skating."

"Ah…you sure? I don't want anything to happen…"

"I'm…pretty sure. Hell. I don't know anything about being pregnant. But even if I fell, I don't think that would do anything at this stage. I'll Google it tomorrow."

He laughed. "Yeah, we better Google lots of things. Including sex."

She huffed out a laugh. "Oh, I think we know how to do that."

"I mean, is it okay to have sex when you're pregnant."

"Oh my god. Even you can't be that clueless."

He grinned. "So that means it's okay? I sure hope so."

"Let me show you."

They moved into the bedroom. When Tag went to turn her and lower her to the bed, she resisted and, smiling, gave him a little shove onto the bed. She climbed on after him, moving over him. She knelt above him and leaned down to kiss him. Their mouths met in a deep, slow tongue kiss.

He reached for her, sliding one hand around to her back and the other down over her hip, her ass, right to her thigh, pulling it up so she stretched out over him, straddling him. Both his hands skimmed down to her ass cheeks, slipping inside her flannel pants, pulling her against him, their mouths still joined. She rubbed her body up and down over his, sending sparks shooting through her veins. She cupped his face, kissed him again. And again. His hands caressed up and down her back.

She made a soft moaning noise, pleasure pouring all through her, turning her body liquid. "Tag," she whispered, his stubbled jaw rough beneath her palm. "I love you."

Then he sat up, pushing her up too, so they were sitting with her straddling his lap. He slid his hands up her torso, pushing her

T-shirt up, up, and she lifted her arms to let him remove it. Her breasts were right in his face and he paused to study them for a moment. Her nipples tightened and heat spread through her, excitement clawing inside her. He wrapped his arms around her and brought her breast to his mouth. He closed his lips around one nipple, his eyes falling shut, one hand covering her ass. Her own hands landed on his hard thighs to brace herself and her head fell back.

"Oh god!" Sensation sizzled from nipple to womb, her pussy aching with a sharp, desperate need. She rocked her body against his as he suckled at her breast, drawing her nipple deep then licking tenderly all over her breast. He moved to the other, and her body quivered with desire.

"Fuck," he murmured against her flesh. "I love your breasts, Kyla. So sweet."

He gently plumped them with his hands, staring down at them. Then he looked back up at her. She nodded, knowing what he was thinking. She threaded her hands through his hair. "They're going to change," she whispered.

"That's okay. I love them. I love you." He bent his head again and another thrill rippled through her body.

She pushed him down to his back again, still straddling him, then moved so she had only one of his thighs between her legs and reached for the thick hard column behind the loose flannel pants. She rubbed him and up and down through the fabric. "Oh," she whispered. "You're so big. I love your cock."

A groan swelled from his throat. Their gazes fastened on each other. Heat built. Nibbling her bottom lip, she pulled his pants down to free his erection. His thick length sprang out and up, and more heat spiraled down to her core. He helped push the pajama pants down his thighs, and she shifted a bit lower on the bed. She bent her head to his groin, crouching there, her butt in the air. Her mouth watered.

His head went back into the pillows, chin lifted. His cock lay along his belly, flushed, rigid, veins pulsing. Mmm. She dragged her tongue up the length of his shaft, around the head, then back down, and tongued his balls. Then she slowly kissed her way back up, opening her mouth over the side, licking, gently sucking. She caught his cock in one hand to lift it up to her mouth and then closed her lips over the head. She sucked him in, swirled her tongue around the smooth rim, then sucked him in again.

He tasted so delicious, so exciting, so male. She murmured her appreciation and swallowed. His thigh tensed beneath hers. "So good," she whispered.

His head lifted and their eyes met as her hair fell around her face and trailed over his abdomen. Using hand and mouth, her gaze fastened on his face, she moved on him. Then she lifted her mouth to smile at him as she stroked her wet hand up and down his shaft.

He smiled back, his eyes dark, his jaw tight. "So good," he rasped. "Fuck, Kyla."

She took him deeper, as deep as she could, her nose almost brushing his lower abdomen. Then she clasped him with both hands as she licked and sucked his balls again. His chest and belly heaved.

His hand came to the back of her head and tangled in her hair, holding her there. He groaned. "Love your mouth on me...so hot...suck me..."

She breathed in the male scent of him, all warm and musky. Her pussy clenched with need.

Then he pulled on her head, pulling her up and over him. She leaned up and kissed him, now with her feet pushing into the mattress, her butt in the air, and he shoved her pajama pants down her legs. She tried to toe them off the rest of the way, but they got hung up on her ankles.

Tag smiled and moved from under her, going to his knees to pull her flannel pants off her ankles and feet. He yanked his own T-shirt off over his head and tossed it aside.

Then as she lay on her side, he bent his head to her ass, crouched there beside her, finding her pussy from behind. "Oh god!" That was so frickin' hot!

His mouth on her sent exquisite pleasure rippling through her, his tongue licking, his lips sucking, his teeth nibbling her ass so gently. She wiped a hand over her wet mouth, turned to watch him with his face buried at her ass. Her insides did a flip and her insides quivered. She bit her lip on a groan and turned away. His big hands cupped her butt and spread her cheeks for his tongue.

Oh god. Oh god. Flames licked over her flesh as his mouth and tongue moved on her, her pussy quivering and melting against his mouth. Her fingers curled into the bed covers, and then he lifted one leg up and over so she was flat on her back with her thighs spread for him.

Still holding her butt cheeks in both hands, he lifted her pussy to his mouth, and, eyes fastened on hers, drew his tongue up her slit in a long, luscious stroke. She covered her breasts and gently squeezed, her body clenching and writhing. She lifted one hand behind her head to support it so she could watch him eating her with slow, deliberate licks and gentle nibbles. He sucked softly on her sex lips. Pressure stretched up her spine and she twisted against his touch. Her other hand lifted to her mouth and she sucked on a finger.

"That's so fucking hot," he groaned. He moved his hand so he could caress her inner thigh, and shivers cascaded over her at the touch on the sensitive skin there. He opened his mouth wider over her pussy, his eyes falling closed. She watched as he slowly slid one long finger inside her. She clenched around him, hips lifting, the ache intensifying low down inside her.

A moan climbed up her throat. He opened his mouth on her pussy in long, devouring kisses, his tongue stroking slowly over her flesh. His big hand rested on her inner thigh, holding it down, and her hips began to lift to his mouth, faster and faster, soft little moans and whimpers filling the room. His tongue moved faster on her clit. Sensation gathered, coiling deep inside her, and she reached for his head with both hands and held him. Her abdominal muscles tensed, her pelvis lifted and then wave after wave after wave of heat crashed through her. She shuddered violently and he continued to eat at her, drawing her orgasm out almost unbearably.

When the storm had eased, he lifted her thigh across her body as he shifted up, kissing her butt cheek, her hip, her stomach, then closing his mouth over a nipple again. Her body pulsed and vibrated, her hand between her now closed thighs cupping her pulsing pussy.

His hand curved over her jaw and brought her mouth to his for another long, scorching kiss. Their mouths hovered a breath apart as he reached for his cock and found her entrance from behind. On her back, her hips twisted forward, they faced each other. Their tongues came out and licked at each other, eyes focused on each other, and he pressed inside her. His hand molded to her butt cheek again, rubbing here there, sliding down her thigh to her knee then back up. Moving inside her, foreheads pressed together, noses side by side, he rocked inside her body. Still sensitive from the orgasm, more pleasure rushed through her, heating her veins.

He cupped the side of her neck his thumb rubbing along her jaw and cheek. His mouth found hers again in a deep, reaching kiss she felt all the way to her pussy. He moved faster and faster. Her fingers still trapped between her thighs found her clit, but she couldn't get the right kind of pressure on it in that position, and she moaned with frustration.

"Okay," he murmured against her mouth, and he turned her body so she was on her stomach on the bed, his cock still embedded in her pussy. On his knees, he lifted her hips, pulling her farther back onto his cock. She braced herself on the bed, gasping, going onto her hands and knees. Hands on her hips, he drove in and out.

"Oh my god," she cried. "That's so deep." He touched so far inside her it almost hurt, with a delicious, exquisite pain. She turned to look at him over her shoulder, reached a hand back to touch him and he slid an arm around her front, hand up to her throat, holding her like that as he drove into her from behind. Her arm slid around the back of his neck, then lowered to cover his on her throat.

"Love you, Kyla," he growled in her ear. "Love you so much."

"Oh Tag."

"You're mine," he added, his fingers tightening on her body. "Mine."

"Yes."

The he lowered his hand to the bed, both of them now on hands and knees. His mouth opened on her back, his tongue lingering warm and wet there. Then he rose back onto his knees, hands gripping her hips. She slid a hand between her legs, now able to find her clit and rub it with greedy abandon, seeking another orgasm. Her orgasm unfurled from the very center of her, rolling outward, every nerve ending tingling, her body going weak and limp. His driving strokes pushed her to the mattress, face pressing into the pillow. He followed her down to kiss her cheek, nuzzle her hair, his breath harsh in her ear. "Fuck yeah. Love how you come on my cock. Tightening around me." And his body went still and taut, his hands gripping her hips, holding her tight against his groin as he pulsed and flooded her with heat.

She could hear his ragged breathing, felt his hands gradually relax and then smooth over her hips. Then he withdrew and stretched out over her, his body damp and hot. "God, Kyla."

"See. We can still have sex."

She felt his smile against her hair. "Can we ever."

CHAPTER TEN

Remi woke up alone Christmas morning in Jase's bedroom. She rolled over and buried her face in the pillow. It didn't even smell like him. A heavy wave of sadness rolled over her that they were fighting and had slept apart. And it was Christmas.

She had the sublet agreement for her apartment folded up in a box and wrapped, which was going to be her gift to him. Moving in with him. It was a sucky present in a way, but it was what he'd wanted and she'd thought it would be a cute way to tell him. But now…now, her stomach cramped at the realization that she'd sublet her apartment and things between them were so awful, he might not even want her to move in anymore. She might be homeless in a month.

Crap.

Pain sliced through her at that thought, the idea of him living in her old home without her unbearable. She loved him. She did want to live with him. She did want to have his babies. Just not right now. Why couldn't he understand that? Why couldn't he wait for her? Why did he have to go running back to his old girl-friend and her baby?

She wanted to go home. But she was stuck in Winnipeg, stuck

there in the Heller home until tomorrow night when they flew back to Chicago.

She sighed. She'd cried last night before she'd fallen asleep and her eyes felt swollen and gritty. She dragged herself out of bed and popped across the hall to the bathroom to wash her face and brush her teeth. She returned to get dressed and found Jase there, digging around in his suitcase, wearing a pair of black boxer briefs. She took a few seconds to admire his body, the solid muscles of his back, the lines of his quadriceps defined in the crouched position.

"Morning," she said quietly.

He glanced at her over his shoulder. The scruff of whiskers was so sexy, but his eyes were deeply shadowed. "Morning."

"Merry Christmas." She tried for some enthusiasm, but it didn't quite come off.

"Yeah. Merry Christmas." He straightened, holding a pair of jeans and a black turtleneck sweater. He proceeded to step into the jeans and then pull the sweater over his head.

Her heart clenched at how gorgeous he looked, ruffled hair, stubbled jaw, sad mouth and all. She moved to her own suitcase.

She pulled out a pair of black leggings and a long red sweater.

"I'll see you downstairs," Jase said gruffly, and disappeared. She sighed.

She quickly dressed and wrapped a big leopard-print scarf around her neck to finish off. Then she needed to add a little makeup to her pale face, trying to disguise the bags under her eyes and puffy eyelids. And what the hell, it was Christmas, so she swiped on bright red lip gloss.

Her stomach swooped as she descended the stairs, admiring the garland that adorned the oak banister. The smell of coffee and something cinnamon-y teased her senses.

She headed toward the voices in the kitchen and great room, where Jase's parents, Nicole and Logan, and Jase and Matt had already congregated.

"Merry Christmas, Remi!" Laura moved toward her and gave her a big hug. "Would you like coffee?"

Remi blinked at the emotion that rose in her at Jase's mom's hug. God. She could use a mom to talk to. Or a friend. Delise was far away, and she wasn't going to be having a girl talk with Nicole.

"I'd love some coffee," she said, forcing a smile. "What smells so good?"

"Homemade cinnamon buns," Laura said. "They're just resting until Tag and Kyla get here. Then we can start opening gifts." She grinned, and it made her look youthful and pretty. "I love presents."

Remi smiled. "Doesn't everyone?"

The sound of the front door opening reached their ears and Laura perked up. A worried crease appeared between her eyes. Remi knew she was thinking about the big announcement yesterday and the way Kyla had rushed out. Remi held her mug in both hands and sipped her hot coffee as Laura rushed to the front door to greet them.

Everyone else fell silent. They couldn't hear the conversation happening out front, only voices. It seemed to take forever, but then Laura appeared again, beaming. God. She honestly glowed with happiness and she headed straight to her husband and slid her arms around his waist and hugged him. Then she tipped her head back and looked up at him and said, "It's true. We're going to be grandparents."

Doug smiled down at her and the joy on their faces made Remi's heart squeeze. She flicked a glance at Jase, and he had a sort of glum smile on his face.

"And they have more news too," Laura added.

Tag and Kyla appeared, and wow, they were both beaming too. Obviously they'd made up whatever fight they'd been having. Remi's mood dipped again at the contrast with what was happening with her and Jase.

"They're engaged!" Laura announced joyfully. "Show them your ring, Kyla!"

Kyla grinned and obediently held out her left hand as everyone crowded around. Hugs and kisses were exchanged, and Remi forced herself to participate, smile firmly in place. She was happy for them, of course she was. How could you be down when surrounded by such joy and love?

Her heart remained heavy though.

She looked at Jase just as he looked at her, and his pained expression mirrored her own feelings. They had to fix this. Obviously, it wasn't going to happen just then.

"Okay, let's have breakfast," Laura said. "Cinnamon buns and fruit salad. And mimosas!"

Yay. Alcohol might help. Remi kept her smile firmly in place as everyone filled their plates and Laura poured mimosas and one glass of straight orange juice for Kyla, and they all moved into the great room, everyone finding a spot to sit.

"When the boys were young, they handed out the presents," Laura said. "So you boys can do that now."

"Boys," Tag snorted, but with a smile.

"There aren't as many presents as there used to be," Matt complained.

"You're not children anymore," his father returned. "The gifts get more expensive as you get older. And anyway, what the hell are we supposed to buy for you guys? You're all frackin' millionaires."

"My problem exactly," Remi couldn't help adding. "Jase wanted a Ferrari. As if."

"Buy your own fucking Ferrari," Logan said, moving to the tree to pick up some gifts and hand them out.

Everyone laughed.

"That's what I told him," Remi said, smiling. "Well, not in those exact words." She sipped her orange juice and champagne and glanced at Jase, whose mouth had curved into a slight smile.

Yeah, it was hard to be down around so much love and happiness.

"You guys should be buying *us* a truckload of expensive presents," Doug added. "With all the money you make."

"Um. I think they did," Laura said, surveying all the gifts that were being piled around her.

"*I'm* not a millionaire," Matt complained. "Far from it. Poor college student here."

Remi smiled at him. He seemed to handle being the baby of the family pretty well. No doubt it was hard to follow behind all these superstars.

Soon gifts were piled at her feet as the four brothers pulled all the presents out from under the tree.

"We usually take turns opening presents," Laura said. "If that's okay with everyone. When the boys were little we couldn't hold them back. They dove in and the place was pretty much trashed with gift wrap and packaging and we never knew who gave what. As they got older, we tried to make them slow down and appreciate each gift."

These boys had been raised right. Remi'd always known it. Jase was solid and grounded, not an asshole superstar. This was why. And this was why family was important to him. A soft warmth swelled in her chest.

They spent the next few hours leisurely opening presents, exclaiming and appreciating each gift. And as Remi picked up her last present to open it, she realized she had no gift from Jase. And her gift for him was still upstairs buried beneath the clothes in her suitcase.

Her insides went cold and her fingers stiffened as she undid the ribbon on the package she held, which turned out to be Crème de la Mer body lotion from Logan and Nicole. "Oh my gosh," she murmured, looking at it. "This is beautiful."

"Enjoy," Nicole said with a hesitant smile.

Remi bit her lip. This was very expensive skin cream that

she'd once tried and loved but couldn't bring herself to spend that much money on. "Thank you."

"Okay," Logan said loudly. "Last present. Go ahead, Nic."

Remi blinked and looked over where Nicole sat in an armchair in the corner. The sun had come out today, reflecting light off the fresh snow out in the yard and illuminating the room through all the big windows, gleaming off Nicole's long blonde hair. Nicole picked up the big parcel and gave it a gentle shake with a questioning look at Logan.

"From me," he confirmed, smiling. He sat back in the chair next to her.

"It's heavy," she murmured. "And…jingling." She pulled open the ribbon then peeled off the heavy red and gold paper. A brown cardboard box remained, and she opened the flaps. Her forehead creased as she dug around in a bunch of Styrofoam popcorn and pulled out a ring of sleigh bells. She held them up. "Um. Thank you."

"That's not all," Logan said, lounging in his chair, smiling.

"Okay." She dug more and pulled out a small package wrapped in tissue. She removed the tissue to reveal a Christmas ornament. "Oh. It's so pretty." She looked at Logan and smiled. "I love it."

"There's more," he said.

She grimaced and dug into the box, pulling out a paperback book. "*Fifty Shades of Grey?*" She lifted an eyebrow.

The rest of the family burst into laughter, Tag collapsing back into the couch cushions. Even Remi had to grin. She snuck a glance at Laura and Doug, who appeared to be trying to conceal their mirth, Laura's hand in front of her mouth, Doug's eyes twinkling.

"I heard it was good," Logan said with a shrug and a smirk. "But that's not all."

Nicole pawed around more in the box but came up empty handed. "There's nothing else."

"Check the ornament," Logan suggested.

Frowning, she held up the small red glass ball, then she peered closer. "*Oh mon dieu.*"

Remi leaned forward, curious. The rest of the family exchanged glances and Remi heard murmurs.

Nicole looked at Logan. "Seriously?"

"Serious as a dislocated shoulder."

The look they shared was incendiary. What…?

Nicole sat there, staring at the ornament. Everyone shifted in their seats, looking at each other. Then she used her fingers to pull something off the top of the ornament, over the golden string that was to hang it. She held up something Remi couldn't quite make out, and then Logan launched out of his chair and went to his knees on the floor in front of Nicole. He took the object from Nicole's fingers and everyone in the room gasped. Realization struck Remi as Logan picked up Nicole's left hand and slid the ring onto her finger. "Well?" he murmured. "Will you marry me?"

Nicole stared at him wordlessly. She glanced down at her finger then back up at Logan. "Logan," she whispered. "It's too soon…"

His smile faded. "No, it's not."

Nicole sent an anxious glance around the room, at everyone staring at her. Her cheeks reddened and she blinked rapidly.

Remi shifted in her chair. Clearly Nicole was uncomfortable with doing this in front of the family. Damn, those Heller boys had a knack for putting their women on the spot. Except for Jase, who hadn't even given her a present. But this was beautiful. Logan reached out to cup Nicole's face. "I love you," he whispered. "Marry me."

Nicole's eyes closed and then opened. She stared into Logan's eyes. "Yes."

He grabbed her and hauled her forward, hugging her, his face pressed to her breast. She wrapped her arms around his head and laid her cheek on top of it.

"Woohoo!" Matt yelled. "Another one bites the dust!"

Everyone laughed and Nicole and Logan pulled apart to smile at each other, a glimmer of tears on Nicole's cheeks.

Remi steadfastly avoided looking at Jase, instead staring fixedly down into her mimosa, a determined smile on her face.

Wow. First Kyla and Tag. Now Logan and Nicole.

Her throat tightened and she took another quick sip of her drink. The she rose out of her chair as everyone crowded around Nicole to congratulate her. She gave Nicole a hug, a bright smile on her face. "Congratulations!" she said. "This is so amazing!"

Nicole nodded, her own smile tightening as she accepted Remi's good wishes. "Thank you."

"Okay, it's time for champagne without the orange juice!" Laura said, making her way through a sea of crumpled wrapping paper and ribbons. "We definitely have a lot to celebrate!"

Remi helped pour champagne, smiled and laughed and toasted. Then she helped Laura with the turkey. Laura had made the stuffing the night before and the two of them filled the turkey's cavities and wrestled the enormous bird into the oven to roast for the rest of the day.

Remi watched in amusement as Laura sprayed bleach cleaner over the entire kitchen. "Stand back," she said. "This will wreck your clothes." She caught Remi's eye. "I'm paranoid, aren't I?"

"Not at all." Remi wiped a counter down. "I do exactly the same. My parents were doctors. They used to joke that we didn't want Uncle Sam and Aunt Ella come to visit." She paused. "Sam and Ella."

"Salmonella." Laura leaned against the counter, laughing. "That's beautiful." She looked at Remi. "Do you miss your parents at Christmas?"

Remi nodded. "Yeah. I do. And this is the first year I've been apart from my brother and sister."

"It's hard when kids grow up and go their separate ways. We've had a few Christmases where the boys weren't here and it's hard. I know Kyla's sad that her parents are in Vancouver this year with Scott."

"But you all are like a second family to her."

"True." Laura glanced at Remi and then paused. "And we're your family now too, Remi. I hope you know that."

Remi's eyes inexplicably filled with tears. But she smiled. "Of course. Thank you."

"What's wrong, sweetheart?" Laura moved closer, a notch between her eyebrows.

"Nothing."

"Remi. I've had a feeling something's been bothering you ever since you got here yesterday. Do you want to talk about it?"

Remi eyed Laura with a mix of longing and apprehension. How could she express her fears about what was happening with her and Jase? With his mother? Putting them into words made them more real. Or maybe it would make them less real. Confusion swirled inside her.

She cast a glance across the room where Jase and his brothers and his dad were all talking about hockey, bursts of laughter filling the air periodically.

"Jase…" She had to stop and swallow, her throat closing up. "Jase is really not taking this news about Brianne's baby well."

Laura nodded, her mouth soft and sad. "Yeah. I got that. He's disappointed."

"So are you."

Laura nodded, lifting one slim shoulder. "Yes. I was disappointed. But it is what it is. And I know this is so much better for the two of you, not to have that to deal with. I'm happy for you two."

"Tag and Kyla's news makes up for that." Remi smiled.

Laura tipped her head. "Well. In a way. But…in another way, no." Her forehead creased. "It's not that I just want grandchildren.

I mean, I do. But mostly, I just want my kids to be happy. So Jase…" Laura fixed a shrewd gaze on her. "He's not taking it well…are you upset for him?"

Something inside Remi shriveled up. She bit her lip. Jeez, she was a selfish bitch. "Um. Yeah. I feel for him." Then she took a deep breath. "But it's more than that. He's got this idea that *we* should have a baby now."

Laura's eyes widened. "Oh."

Remi nodded. "But I…I don't want to. I mean, right now. I do want kids. Some day. This just isn't…a good time. For me. God." She groaned and leaned on the counter, head in her hands. "I'm so selfish."

Laura's hand landed on her back in a gentle touch. "No you're not. You get a say in when you have kids. Of course you do."

"Thank you. Could you tell Jase that?"

"I certainly will."

"No! I didn't mean that! I was joking."

"I'll talk to him, Remi. If you want. Maybe he needs to be smacked upside the head."

"I don't want to make trouble. We need to work things out. But it's causing a lot of tension between us. He…he went to see Brianne and the baby the other day."

Remi peeked up at Laura, whose eyes clouded. "Oh."

"I was scared," Remi whispered.

"You have nothing to worry about," Laura said, patting her back. "Jase loves you. I know he does."

"I-it doesn't feel like it right now. He d-didn't even give me a Christmas present."

"What?" Laura frowned.

Remi shrugged and straightened. "It's okay. We'll talk. It's just…this isn't a good time. So much family around and other things going on."

Laura nodded. "That's true. If you two want to take off by yourselves, just do it."

"Jase is really looking forward to going to the community center this afternoon."

And in fact the others were starting to talk about going down there, rising out of chairs. It was already well past noon and it was a beautiful blue and white Christmas day outside.

"Okay," Laura said. "Let's go." She slid an arm around Remi's shoulders and hugged her. "It'll be okay."

Sure. Sure it would.

CHAPTER ELEVEN

However crappy Jase was feeling, he knew skating and playing hockey was a great way to deal with it. Nothing made him happier than lacing on skates and getting on the ice. Okay, well almost nothing. Remi made him happier. Usually.

He shook those thoughts off as he skated slowly backwards on the ice at the community center. The air was hard and cold, but breathing it in felt so good, sharp and clean. He watched as the rest of the family followed him onto the rink, Remi's skating smooth like a figure skater, Nicole's fast and aggressive in her hockey skates, Kyla's cautious. Mom and Dad even joined them, although Mom said she didn't want to leave the house empty for too long with the turkey in the oven.

He watched as Tag kept a careful eye on Kyla, watched Logan and Nicole passing the puck between them, grinning at each other as the passes grew faster and harder. That was cool, watching them together on the ice like that, Nicole's hockey talent obvious. It was in her genes, clearly.

This should make him the happiest guy in the world, seeing everyone together like this, the winter sun shining so brightly on them in the clear blue sky, sparkling off the pure white banks of snow piled around the outside of the boards. The scrape of blades on ice, the crack of the puck on a stick or thunking against the boards filled the air, along with laughter and teasing trash talk between his brothers.

But he wasn't the happiest guy in the world.

He thought about the present he had for Remi, back at the house, the present he'd been too afraid to give her. Fuck, he was chickenshit.

The puck Matt passed to him slid right by him.

"Dude, wake up!" Matt called.

"Yeah yeah."

A little kid skated up to Tag and stopped and stared. "Are you Tag Heller?"

Tag grinned. "I sure am."

"Holy moly!" The kid's mouth dropped open and he turned. "Dad! C'mere! It's Tag Heller."

"And my brothers are here too," Tag said. "Logan and Jason, and Matt."

The little guy's eyes went wide. His call had attracted attention from a few other kids and parents who'd arrived at the rink. "Jason Heller! Can I get your autograph?"

"Sure," Jase said with a smile. "But what do you want me to sign?"

"Um...my hockey stick?"

Jase had nothing with him, not even a stub of a pencil. And then Remi glided over to him, holding out a black Sharpie. "Never go out without it," she murmured.

Christ. She was amazing. He shot her a look of gratitude and took the pen.

For the next while, all four brothers were busy signing sticks and anything else people could find for them to autograph, and chatting with fans. The girls bailed on them right away, heading back to the house with Mom. No way would any of the Hellers let down their fans, though, and hell, it was fun. They got back to shooting the puck around a bit, and Jase knew they'd made a bunch of kids' Christmases pretty special by getting to play hockey with the Heller brothers.

Then a CBC news reporter and camera guy showed up. Someone had apparently called the local television station to tell them what was happening. Again, Jase couldn't be annoyed. It was cool. So they stayed a little longer while they filmed them all there, even following them inside the club house where Tag bought everyone hot chocolate, the middle-aged dad volunteer who was manning the concession stand grinning like a fool at all the excitement. He'd have quite a story to tell.

How many times did this happen, where all four of them were together like this? Not very damn many. It was pretty fucking awesome.

Eventually they headed home, the sun low in the winter sky, casting long shadows across snowy streets. Jase and Tag followed a little behind Logan and Matt and Dad, their footsteps crunching in hard snow.

"So. What was the drama yesterday with Kyla?" Jase asked. "She didn't want you to tell anyone she's pregnant?"

"Nope." Tag grimaced. "Actually, she wasn't sure she wanted to have the baby."

Jase blinked. Whoa. "Really?" he asked slowly. He thought, with some shame, of the spear of jealousy he'd felt when he'd heard the news.

Tag nodded, a glum smile lifting one corner of his mouth. "Yeah. It's not a good time for her, career-wise. Plus she didn't like the surprise of it. She likes to plan things."

"So you didn't plan this."

"Total accident." Tag sighed. "She just did a pregnancy test the day before yesterday. Fuck, she was upset. I fucking *hated* seeing her like that."

"Oh man. I'm sorry."

"It's okay. We talked. She's good with it now. Or getting there, anyway." He eyed Jase. "You relieved Brianne's baby isn't yours?"

Jase didn't answer at first. People kept asking him that, and he knew he should be, but no, it wasn't relief he'd been feeling. But now it felt kind of shitty to say that. "I'd gotten used to the idea of being a father," he finally said.

"Scares the shit outta me," Tag confessed. "I don't know how you were dealing with it. But hey. The good thing is, you and Remi can have kids of your own some day, without the complication of Brianne in your lives. Way better for you two. You can talk about it together and plan, not have it sprung on you like Brianne did. I mean, I'm happy. I'm thrilled. But you know, it's a big thing."

Jase nodded slowly. Yeah. It was a big thing.

Back at the house, Nicole and the other women unwrapped themselves from scarves and jackets and gathered in the kitchen.

"What needs to be done, Laura?" Kyla asked, sweeping her long dark hair behind her shoulders.

Remi envied her easy comfort in the Heller kitchen.

Laura opened the oven door and began to baste the turkey. "We need to peel the potatoes. I've got green beans that need to be trimmed and carrots to peel and cut up."

"It smells amazing," Nicole said. She opened the big refrigerator and pulled out a crisper drawer. "Here are the beans and carrots. Where are the potatoes?"

"They're sitting on the counter over there." Laura nodded.

Remi grabbed the big bag of potatoes.

"I think we should have a glass of wine while we work," Laura said. "Except you, Kyla. Oh my god." She paused as she lifted a bottle of white wine out of the fridge. "Kyla. You're pregnant."

Kyla grinned. "Apparently. I know. I can't believe it either."

Laura just stood there for a moment, so obviously emotional, and Remi's throat ached a little bit. What would that be like, to feel that way? To have someone so thrilled that you were pregnant, to be bringing another life—another Heller—into the world?

Well. She could easily find out. If she'd done what Jase wanted, they could soon be telling everyone they were having a baby too.

It was tempting, but that was the wrong reason to have a baby. And now… She looked down at the potato in her hand with blurry vision. Maybe she didn't even have that choice anymore.

"You seem so happy now," Nicole remarked to Kyla. "Yesterday not so much. I'm kind of embarrassed to admit I thought it was because you hated me."

Kyla paused. "Oh no! I'm so sorry, Nicole. Of course I don't hate you. I was really distracted yesterday. The truth is…we didn't plan this. I guess you all figured that out. I'd actually told Tag that I wasn't sure…" She swallowed. "I wasn't sure if I wanted the baby."

All the women made sympathetic murmurs.

"It's okay, now," Kyla continued with a smile. "I'm still freaked out about it and I'm still not sure what's going to happen with my job when they find out. But whatever." She shrugged. "We're having a baby and the world will just have to deal with it."

"They won't fire you?" Remi asked with shock.

"No, of course not. It's a law firm. They would know that would get their asses sued for wrongful dismissal." Kyla chuckled. "It's just that it's an old boys' club law firm that doesn't have much belief in work-life balance. But you know. One woman at a time, I'm working on changing that. Thanks to Tag. And Jesus, if they can't deal with it, I'll just quit." She shrugged. "There's nothing more important than family."

"Amen," Laura said quietly. "I'm so glad to hear you say that.

Not that your career isn't important too, but you were making yourself sick."

"Your son," Kyla said pointedly. "Thank him. And thank you, Laura, for making him the man he is." She blinked.

"My goodness, we're a sappy bunch today," Laura said, lifting her wine glass.

"Hey, it's not often this whole family gets together," Kyla said. "You're entitled to be emotional."

"Especially since two of my boys are getting married. And Tag's going to be a dad."

Remi lowered her head again, sadness washing through her. Then Laura's hand landed on her shoulder.

"Remi. Don't feel bad."

"No pressure at all," she choked out. She too picked up her wine and took a big gulp.

"What pressure?" Kyla asked. Remi glanced at her. Kyla's head tilted and her forehead creased.

Remi sighed. "Jase wants a baby."

"Oh." Kyla blinked. "Wasn't he relieved to find out Brianne's baby isn't his?"

Remi told them what had happened in a halting voice. "I feel like I'm letting everyone down," she ended shakily. "Like I'm the most selfish bitch in the world for not wanting to have a baby right now."

"Oh my god." Kyla stepped up and hugged her. Remi's eyes watered helplessly. "*You* decide when it's right for you. I didn't have a choice and that pissed me off so much. I mean, I'm accepting it now, and it'll be fine, but don't let anyone pressure you into doing something you don't want to."

"I do want it," Remi choked out. "I love babies and kids. Just not right now. And now things are s-such a mess with me and Jase...I'm af-fraid..." She couldn't even say it.

"It'll be okay," Kyla soothed and Laura clucked with dismay.

"Th-thank you. But he's so obsessed with having a baby..."

She hesitated to say it out loud, her deepest fear that she hadn't even been able to fully admit to herself. "I'm afraid he's going to go back to Brianne."

Everyone went silent.

"That's crazy," Kyla breathed.

"I know. I know it is! But it's what I'm afraid of."

"Oh, Remi."

Remi lifted her head from Kyla's shoulder and stepped back. Laura handed her a tissue. She smiled and wiped her eyes. "I'm so sorry. This is such a happy time for both of you." She looked at Nicole and Kyla. "I don't want to ruin your beautiful Christmas."

Nicole looked back at her and took a deep breath. "Well, since I already admitted I was an idiot thinking Kyla hated me, I'll confess I thought you hated me too when I met you yesterday." One corner of her mouth lifted. "Now I feel bad, because I can see you were upset about something else entirely."

"Oh no." Remi's chest tightened. "I'm so sorry, Nicole. I've been all wrapped up in my own stuff. Of course I don't hate you!"

"I sound like a neurotic narcissist or something," Nicole said with a laugh. "Honestly, I don't really think everything is about me."

"Does it have anything to do with what happened with Cody Burrell?" Laura asked.

Silence fell in the room.

"Just putting it out there," Laura added. "Sorry to bring it up."

Remi looked at Nicole. "I'd forgotten about that whole shit storm. That must have been awful for you."

Nicole's ex-boyfriend, a defenseman for the Minnesota Caribou, had basically trashed her on national television by implying she'd slept her way through the entire team.

"It was pretty horrendous. My self esteem took a beating. I swore I would never date another hockey player again after that. But..." She smiled. "Logan was very persistent."

Remi's heart softened. "I'm sorry, Nicole," she said again. "I was looking forward to meeting you and getting to know you. I mean, I don't even know Logan that well yet…" Her voice trailed off. She was still so afraid that things might be done between her and Jase, that she never would have a chance to get to know Logan better, or Nicole, or meet Kyla and Tag's baby… A wrench of regret shook her. Her fingers gripped the edge of the granite counter. "Anyway, I'm sorry I was acting so bitchy."

"Don't worry about it." Nicole smiled. "You've got other things on your mind."

"You're so gorgeous," Remi said with a wry grin. "Perfect bone structure, flawless skin…tall and thin. You make me feel like a little schlub."

Nicole laughed. "A what?"

"A schlub." Remi shrugged. "I might've just made that word up. But you get my drift."

"You're the one who makes me feel like a big awkward giant," Nicole said. "You're so tiny and pretty."

"Oh you girls," Laura said, swiping at one eye. "You're all gorgeous. All of you. On the inside and the outside. I am the luckiest mom in the world."

"Let's have a group hug," Kyla suggested, and the emotion thickening the room dissipated as they all laughed.

They'd had several glasses of wine and had set the big dining room table, dinner almost all ready, before the guys all showed up, stomping and tramping into the house, letting in a blast of cold air.

"God, that smells good!" Tag called. "Is it ready?"

"Almost," his mom said. "Where the heck have you been?"

"Having fun."

Remi eyed them all, red-cheeked, sparkling-eyed, wide smiles.

"A bunch of kids showed up and wanted to play with us," Jase said. "And then CBC showed up to film us, and it was really fun."

"Well, dinner will be ready soon, so get cleaned up and get back down here."

"Yes, ma'am."

They all trooped upstairs. Remi carried more wineglasses to the dining room and set them on the table while Nicole lit the big candle in the centerpiece of pine and holly. The flame and low lights in the room sparkled on crystal and silverware and reflected off the dark glass of the window.

"It's so pretty," Nicole said.

Remi glanced at her as she placed a wineglass. "Do you miss your family?"

"A little." She grimaced. "My parents and I aren't that close. Mostly I miss my brother. He lives in Vancouver."

"He plays for the Rockies, right?"

"Yeah."

"Kyla's brother lives in Vancouver too."

"Oh really?"

"But he's not a hockey player." Remi paused, then said quietly, "You and Logan are great together."

"Thank you. We haven't been together long. He blew me away with this ring. It seems really fast. But he said he knew he wanted to be with me the moment he met me."

"Love at first sight."

"For him. If you believe that. It took me a little longer. Like I said, I was determined to never get involved with another hockey player."

"They're all pretty great guys."

"Yeah. Don't worry, Remi. Things will work out for you and Jason."

"Thanks." She smiled but her insides were still knotted.

Soon they were all sitting down to eat. Mrs. Heller dimmed the light hanging above the big table. Darkness had fallen outside the big window and the candle flickered warmly in the middle of the table, sparkling on the glass and silverware. In the background, Christmas music played softly.

It should have been perfect. Remi sat next to Jase, everyone else took their seats, Doug at the head of the table, Laura at the foot.

"I want to say grace," Laura said. "This is a special Christmas, with all of us together and new members of our family."

Others murmured their assent and bowed their heads. Remi's family had never been particularly religious and she hadn't said grace at a meal for a long time, but she appreciated and respected the thought.

"Our Heavenly Father," Laura began. "We thank you for this food, and humbly request that you perform a miracle and remove all the calories from dessert."

Laughter rippled around the table and Remi couldn't help glancing at Jase beside her. Their eyes met in a brief but warm contact. She swallowed.

"Thank you, Father, for the gifts you have given us, not just this food, but the family around us. We are so privileged to have so much. And we are so thankful to have such beautiful new additions to our family—Remi, Nicole and Kyla. And a baby who will join us in the fall, a precious gift. Words can't express how happy we are that our four boys have grown up to be such wonderful men. It amazes me that three of them have found their life partners and have found such wonderful, strong women. Matt, your turn is coming."

More laughter ensued.

"Ball and chain," Matt muttered almost inaudibly, and Tag gave him an elbow in the ribs. "Oomph."

"Just like the old days," Laura said, smiling. "With the boys tussling at the dinner table. Moving on. It makes me and your father happy to know that even though you all have achieved such incredible success, you still have your feet firmly on the ground and realize what the most important things in life are. Family. And love. But I also want to say that family and love are a choice we make. We are blessed to have that, and I'm happy you have chosen that, but we could easily make choices that are different."

Remi caught Kyla's concerned glance at Tag.

"Not you, Kyla," Laura added.

Kyla grimaced.

"What I'm trying to say is, even if you did make choices that were different, if you chose not to marry, or not to have children, or if you wanted to marry a man—"

Roars erupted around the table.

"Hold on—"

"What the fuck?"

"Jesus, Mom, just because I don't have a girlfriend doesn't mean I'm gay!"

Laura held up her hands. "Ssssh. I'm talking."

Everyone fell silent.

Remi had to admire a woman who could control such an unruly bunch of alpha males.

"I'm hungry," Logan muttered.

A few snickers sounded. Laura's lips twitched.

This was the weirdest prayer Remi had ever heard. But she liked it.

"What I am trying to say," Laura said again, "is that your choices are just that—*your choices*. And we love you and support you no matter what. You don't need to give us grandchildren to make us happy. But we will love your children absolutely if and when you have them. We will love your partners if and when you have them—"

"I'm not gay," Matt muttered again.

"Because *you* love them," she continued. "And if you don't have children, that doesn't make you less of a man. Or less of a grownup. Or less of anything. Unless you let it."

Remi jerked as Jase's chair scraped back on the hardwood floor. He hurled his napkin onto the seat.

"Okay. I get it," he snapped. "Thanks a lot."

He stalked out of the dining room.

Laura blinked as her gaze followed him out of the room. She turned back to the others, and said, "Amen."

Remi sat there as the room went silent, everyone staring in astonishment after Jase.

"What crawled up his ass?" Matt muttered.

Remi stared down at her empty plate. Laura's words echoed in her head. *Doesn't make you less of a man. Or less of an adult.*

Oh god. Was that what this was all about? Did Jase seriously feel he had to be a father to be a man? To be a responsible grown up?

Remi lifted her head and blinked. She looked at Laura. "C-can I be excused?" Remi choked out, folding her napkin as she pushed her chair back.

Laura nodded. "Go to him."

CHAPTER TWELVE

Jase sat on the side of the bed in the room he was supposed to share with Remi. Except they'd slept apart last night. And now he had a sick feeling that his stupidity had wrecked everything between them.

His mother's words had ignited a flare of temper inside him, but once he'd walked out of the room, he'd realized the truth of them. He wasn't acting like a grown man. A responsible adult. He was acting like a spoiled child who hadn't got his own way.

He thought about what Tag had said, that at first Kyla wasn't sure she wanted the baby. Tag had been low key about it, but it had obviously bothered him. Yeah, Jase knew what it was like to have a surprise pregnancy. He'd been completely freaked out when Brianne had dumped that on him. He'd be lying if he said he hadn't thought about whether Brianne should go through with the pregnancy. Tag's reaction had been the opposite. But their situation had been entirely different. Tag loved Kyla. Jase had already fallen in love with Remi when he'd learned about Brianne's pregnancy.

Yeah, at that point, he sure hadn't wanted to be a dad. But he'd accepted it. He'd been determined to be honorable and mature about it, after his initial meltdown. But now…he wasn't being honorable and mature. Shame burned inside Jase at how he'd pressured Remi to have a baby. He thought about Kyla, pregnant when she didn't want to be. He thought about the roughness in Tag's voice when he'd talked about how upset Kyla had been. Christ, he didn't want that for Remi!

Yes, unplanned pregnancies happened and yes, you dealt with them the best you could. But when you had a choice, it was a choice you made together.

He'd hurt Remi. He'd never wanted to hurt her. But with selfish blindness he hadn't even seen how his actions were hurtful to her, the woman he loved more than anything. Fuck.

The door opened and Remi peered in. He watched her, his heart heavy and aching. She quietly closed the door behind her. "Jase. I'm so sorry."

His jaw went slack and he frowned. "What are you sorry for? I'm the one who's been acting like an asshole."

She smiled and crossed the room to sit beside him. She reached for one of his big hands. "True. Go ahead and grovel."

A smile tugged at his lips. "I'm sorry. I'm sorry I hurt you. I never intended to do that, but I was being a selfish, self-absorbed jerk. I was all wallowing and feeling sorry for myself and trying to figure out how I could still be a 'real man', and not even thinking about anyone else."

She nodded. "A decent start to groveling."

He closed his eyes and his fingers tightened on hers. "I don't deserve you, Remi. I'm so sorry. I was pushing you to have a baby and I shouldn't have. And I never should have gone to see Emily like that."

"You were worried about her. And I love you for that." She clasped his hand now with both of hers. "I'm sorry too, Jase. I haven't been very understanding of what you've been going through."

"Fuck, Remi. Don't even say that." His insides twisted into knots at her apology, which he didn't deserve.

"I didn't realize how much your whole self-image was wrapped up in being a father."

He sighed. "Yeah. But that was just stupid. As my mom just pointed out to me."

"Huh. I thought she was talking to me." Their eyes met in a warm connection. Hope unfurled inside him as Remi lifted his hand and kissed his knuckles. "It wasn't stupid. I love how you stepped up and took responsibility. I even loved how you believed Brianne, because even though she lied, it said a lot about the kind of man you are that you believed her. Because *you* would never lie or deceive someone that way."

He groaned then shifted to face her. He touched her soft cheek with his fingertips. "Can you forgive me, Remi? I hated sleeping without you last night. I was so worried that my stupidity had destroyed everything. I love you."

Her eyes went glossy. "I love you too, Jase. I was afraid too. I was afraid you wanted a baby so much you'd rather be with Brianne than with me. I kept insisting I wasn't ready for a baby and I was worried I'd driven you away."

"Fuck no." He stared at her. "How could you even think that? You know I have no feelings for Brianne at all. Even I wouldn't be that much of an asshole. And I never should have pressured you about having a baby. You had every right to say no. It's a decision we have to make together."

"Thank you." She squeezed his hand in both her little ones. "You know I want kids some day. I want to have your babies."

His chest went all soft and hot. "Thank you."

"What if…what if it turned out we couldn't have kids?" She looked down at their joined hands and her fingers moved restlessly. "Would you still love me?"

He pulled her onto his lap and wrapped his arms around her. "Christ, yes. And I feel sick that you even have to ask that. I am so sorry, Remi. I love you. I need you. That's all." He found her mouth with his and kissed her, a slow gentle meeting of their mouths. Her body felt so good in his, small and soft and perfect and she tasted like… love.

Their tongues met and nudged, mouths opening wider. His hand found the curve of her ass and pulled her even tighter against him. And then he felt the wetness of her cheek and he drew back. Tears glistened on her cheeks in the lamplight but she smiled at him.

"I love you, Remi."

"Love you too." She traced a finger over his eyebrow. "You are a wonderful man, Jase. You don't need to be a father to prove that. You did the right thing with Brianne and in the end, I am sorry you were disappointed. Even though I'm relieved."

"I know you are. And I know this is for the best. For us. Maybe I could have handled things with Brianne differently. I kind of wish I'd never told my family about it. Then my mom wouldn't have been disappointed too."

"You trusted Brianne. You can't be faulted for that."

"I felt like an idiot. Everyone kept telling me I had to get that paternity test done and I kept insisting we didn't need it. And then in the end…" His mouth twisted. "It was a good thing I did."

"Um. If you're concerned about Emily…how about we go see her together?"

He stared at her, his lips parted, his eyes searching hers. "Christ, Remi. Now I really know I don't deserve you." He crushed her up against him again and held her for a long moment brimming with emotion. He swallowed hard before he spoke. "I have something for you. Your Christmas present."

Her lips quivered. "I wondered why you didn't give me anything. Were you that mad at me?"

"Not exactly." He tipped his head. "More like…afraid. You didn't give me anything either."

"I know. I kind of…chickened out."

One of his eyebrows lifted. "You too, huh."

She slid off his lap and crouched in front of her suitcase on the floor. She pawed around in it and then brought out a small wrapped box with a glittery silver bow on it. "Here," she said.

He took it from her and held it. The box was very light. He slipped the ribbon and bow off then tore open the red paper. Inside the box were some folded papers. *What the...?* He frowned and pulled them out, setting the box aside so he could unfold the papers and read them. "A sublet agreement." He lifted his gaze to her face. Then it dawned on him. "For your apartment?"

"Yes. February first." She nibbled her bottom lip and regarded him with blinking eyes. "I'll be homeless as of that date. I need somewhere to live."

The papers fluttered to the floor as he hauled her back into his arms and kissed her with all the relief and joy sweeping through him. "Thank you, Rem. That's the best present. I want you with me all the time."

"I want to be with you." She drew in a shaky breath. "That's why I was afraid to give it to you. If you didn't want me anymore, I really *would* be homeless. And it's kind of a lame present, since all it cost me was the wrapping paper. But I do have something else for you, back home. Something you couldn't open in front of your parents."

"Ah." He chuckled. "Can't wait." He met her eyes. "You sure about moving in, baby? I know you wanted to be all independent and live your own life for a while."

"Yeah. I did. I do. But like you don't have to be defined by fatherhood, I don't have to be defined by living alone. I can live with you and still be independent. It's not about where I live, it's about being strong with Kyle and Jasmine, and having my own interests. Right?"

His throat squeezed. "Right. You are so right."

"I was being just as stubborn and blind as you were."

"Hey." But he smiled. "Remi, being a hockey wife or girlfriend isn't always easy. There are lots of times I'm travelling when you'll be on your own. I *need* you to be strong and independent."

Her pretty mouth curved into a shaky smile. "I can do that."

He kissed her softly again. "I know you can. Okay, now my turn. Your present's up here too." He sucked a quick breath in and out then lifted Remi off his lap to sit her on the bed. He went to his suitcase and reached beneath some clothes to pull out the tiny package. "It's not wrapped." The husky timbre of his voice surprised him and he cleared his throat. He knelt on the floor in front of her.

"More groveling?" she asked with amusement, reaching out to run her fingers through his hair.

"I hope I don't have to grovel." He opened the box and showed it to her.

Her pretty eyes went huge and her mouth turned into an O of surprise. She blinked, staring. Jase turned the box toward him to make sure the ring was still in fact there. Yep. The big diamond solitaire was sparkling like crazy.

"Will you marry me, Remi? I won't rush you. It can be whenever you want. You can plan whatever kind of wedding you want. Maybe summer would be best."

She gave a strangled little laugh and swatted his shoulder.

"Seriously. This isn't pressure. It's just making it official, that one day we'll be married." His muscles twitched and his heart thudded as he waited for her answer.

"Yes. Yes. I'll marry you."

Air left his lungs all at once and his hands shook a little as he fumbled the ring out of the black velvet lining. He reached for her hand and slid it on. "Perfect," he breathed.

"It's beautiful." She held her hand up to admire it then looked at him. "I love it."

"Thank Christ. I had no clue what I was doing. Delise helped with the size."

"Delise! She knew about this? Why, that sneaky witch…"

Jase laughed and slid his hands to her hips, still kneeling at her feet. Which he would happily do for the rest of his life. "I swore her to secrecy."

"Argh! No wonder she kept telling me how much you care."

"So. Let's have engagement sex," he said hopefully. "Right now."

Remi giggled, her hand in his hair again. "You know I want to. But geez, Jase, your family is all downstairs wondering what the hell is going on. Oh my god, I can't believe we all got engaged! Did you know what the others were doing?"

He shook his head. "Not a clue. Tag and Kyla didn't really surprise me, except I have a feeling that was a last minute decision on Tag's part when they found out she was pregnant. Nicole and Logan…wow. They haven't even known each other that long, but what the heck, they seem perfect together."

"I want to show them my ring!"

He grinned. "Okay. Let's go make everyone's day. Things have been a little tense around here."

He stood and pulled her to her feet, once more hugging her tightly. "I'll try not to be a douchebag again," he whispered. "But if I am, just smack me. Okay?"

"Count on it."

They descended the stairs hand in hand and walked into the dining room like that. The room was full of voices and cutlery clinking against dishes. Everyone had already filled their plates and made a damn good start on eating everything. "There better be turkey left," Jase said.

Everyone went silent and looked at them. He grinned.

The relief in the room was palpable. Jase looked at his mom. "Sorry, Mom. I interrupted your grace."

Snorts and hoots greeted that.

"I was finished," she said calmly. She set down her napkin and rose from her chair to approach them. She eyed Remi. "Okay?"

Remi nodded, blinking her eyes. Jesus, she wasn't going to cry again, was she? She held up her left hand to show Mom.

Mom's eyes nearly popped out and she gasped. "Oh my god!" She grabbed Remi's hand then enfolded her in a bear hug. "I can't believe this! Oh my god!'

Everyone else started talking and chairs rubbed on the floor as people stood and rushed to hug both Jase and Remi.

"Jesus," Matt said loudly. "It's a hat trick."

Everyone laughed and Jase flashed his brother a grin.

Laura shot Jase a narrow-eyed look even as she swiped at a tear. "How did you pull that out of a hat?"

His smile was relaxed. "Didn't. I had it the whole time. Chickened out this morning."

"Oh, Jase." She gave him a light cuff on the side of his head. "That's for being an idiot."

"Ow." He rubbed his head ruefully. "Geez." Then he smiled and met her eyes. "Thanks, Mom."

"Sit, everyone sit, let's finish eating," Mom said, waving her hands. "Maybe I should say grace again, so I can say a special thanks—"

A chorus of no's broke out and she laughed.

"Okay, fine. Just eat."

Jase slid Remi a sideways glance as they took their seats, side by side. He held her gaze for a moment, surrounded by his family. Fuck, he was a lucky sonofabitch. He wanted to be the man Remi thought he was, instead of acting like a cranky toddler. He was *going* to be the man Remi thought he was. He was going to spend the rest of his life making her happy. He'd probably screw up. He sighed as he forked a big piece of turkey onto his plate. But she already knew he wasn't perfect—and she loved him anyway.

~

If you haven't already read the first three Heller Brothers books, be sure to check out

Breakaway (Jase)
Faceoff (Tag)
One Man Advantage (Logan)

ALSO BY KELLY JAMIESON

HELLER BROTHERS HOCKEY

BREAKAWAY

FACEOFF

ONE MAN ADVANTAGE

HAT TRICK

OFFSIDE

POWER SERIES

POWER STRUGGLE

POWER PLAY

POWER SHIFT

RULE OF THREE SERIES

RULE OF THREE

RHYTHM OF THREE

REWARD OF THREE

SAN AMARO SINGLES

WITH STRINGS ATTACHED

HOW TO LOVE

SLAMMED

WINDY CITY KINK

SWEET OBSESSION
ALL MESSED UP
PLAYING DIRTY

BREW CREW
LIMITED TIME OFFER
NO OBLIGATION REQUIRED

ACES HOCKEY
MAJOR MISCONDUCT
OFF LIMITS
ICING
TOP SHELF
BACK CHECK
SLAP SHOT
PLAYING HURT
BIG STICK
GAME ON

LAST SHOT
BODY SHOT
HOT SHOT
LONG SHOT

BAYARD HOCKEY
SHUT OUT
CROSS CHECK

WYNN HOCKEY

PLAY TO WIN

IN IT TO WIN IT

WIN BIG

FOR THE WIN

GAME CHANGER

BEARS HOCKEY

MUST LOVE DOGS…AND HOCKEY

YOU HAD ME AT HOCKEY

TALK HOCKEY TO ME

THE O ZONE

GOOD HANDS

SCORING BIG

MERRY PUCKING CHRISTMAS

STANDALONES

THREE OF HEARTS

LOVING MADDIE FROM A TO Z

DANCING IN THE RAIN

LOVE ME

LOVE ME MORE

2 HOT 2 HANDLE

FRIENDS WITH BENEFITS

LOST AND FOUND

ONE WICKED NIGHT

SWEET DEAL

HOW SWEET IT IS

HOT RIDE

CRAZY EVER AFTER

ALL I WANT FOR CHRISTMAS

SEXPRESSO

NIGHT IRISH SEX FAIRY

CONFERENCE CALL

RIGGER

YOU REALLY GOT ME

SCREWED

FIRECRACKER

BIG WITCH ENERGY

HATE ME UNDER THE MISTLETOE

ABOUT THE AUTHOR

Kelly Jamieson is the bestselling author of over thirty romance novels and novellas. Her writing has been described as "emotionally complex", "sweet and satisfying" and "blisteringly sexy". If she can stop herself from reading or writing, she loves to cook. She has shelves of cookbooks that she reads at length. She also enjoys gardening in the summer, and in the winter she likes to read gardening magazines and seed catalogues (there might be a theme here…) She also loves shopping, especially for clothes and shoes.

Subscribe to her newsletter for updates about her new books and what's coming up.

Find out what's new...
www.kellyjamieson.com
info@kellyjamieson.com